PRIMAL PASSION
TRINITY MASTERS: FALL OF THE GRAND MASTER
BOOK TWO

MARI CARR

LILA DUBOIS

Copyright 2017 by Mari Carr and Lila Dubois

All Rights Reserved.

No part of this book, with the exception of brief quotations for book reviews or critical articles, may be reproduced or transmitted in any form or by any means, electronic or mechanical, including photocopying, recording, or by any information storage and retrieval system without express written permission from the author.

This is a work of fiction. Names, characters, places, and incidents are the product of the author's imagination or are used fictitiously, and any resemblance to actual persons, living or dead, business establishments, events, or locales is entirely coincidental.

Editor: Kelli Collins

Cover artist: Lila Dubois

❋ Created with Vellum

TRIGGER WARNINGS

The Trinity Masters series is a romantic suspense and all books contain explicit sex and depictions of violence (action scenes).

PRIMAL PASSION

An FBI agent. A dominant billionaire. And a virgin scientist.

Deni Parker doesn't have time for anything but her cutting-edge scientific work, and that's how she likes it. So when she's called to the altar—years ahead of what she expected—by the very intimidating, and far too handsome, Price Bennett, Deni's more than a little unprepared.

As CEO of a major security firm and heir to one of the largest fortunes in the world, Price is annoyed when the Grand Master orders him to transport the disorganized scientist to the ceremony to meet her partners. It's only when they arrive that Price realizes he isn't a messenger—he's been matched with Deni.

Gunner Wells has been in love with Deni for years, but he's resisted giving in to his attraction. When he is summoned to be married, he's delighted to discover Deni is not only a member of the secret society, but one of his partners...along with billionaire playboy, Price.

Their strong personalities clash—in and out of the bedroom

—but Price and Gunner have to put aside their overprotectiveness, and Deni must put aside her pride, when someone tries to stop her research—with deadly methods.

Their strong personalities clash—in the bedroom and out of it—but Price and Gunner have to put aside their overprotectiveness, and Deni must put aside her pride, when someone tries to stop her research—with deadly methods.

PROLOGUE

"You asked to see me, Grand Master?"

"Yes. I need you to perform a task, Price."

Price lowered his head in deference. The Grand Master knew it wasn't easy for some members of the Trinity Masters to bend their will to a higher authority. They were a powerful, wealthy, intelligent group of trailblazers, one and all. The man standing before the Grand Master no doubt suffered the most when it came to taking orders. Regardless of that fact, Price had risen to a position of power within the organization because he was confident, driven and trustworthy. In the years since Price had joined the secret society, he'd become one of the Grand Master's most trusted advisors.

Today's venture would test, possibly shatter, that relationship.

"I need you to deliver this summons. The recipient's name and address are on the envelope."

Price's eyes narrowed with annoyance. His knee-jerk reaction was exactly as the Grand Master expected. "Forgive me, sir, but my role in the Trinity Masters does not require me to play messenger."

The Grand Master rose slowly. He'd learned long ago friendship was a luxury he couldn't afford. Regardless, there were times when he missed it. "Your duty is to the Trinity Masters and to me. Are you questioning my authority? And please, be very careful with your response, Mr. Bennett."

Price took a slight step back—no doubt surprised by the genuine threat in his tone. They stared for several moments, each of them sizing up the other, before Price bowed his head once more. "I apologize. I was in a very important meeting when I received your missive to report here at once. I thought there was an emergency. My duty to the Trinity Masters is as it has always been. I will serve. Them...and you."

He noticed how Price hesitated to add the last part. The Grand Master held Price's gaze for a long, silent moment, letting his displeasure over being challenged sink in. Price looked away first.

The Grand Master sat once more. "I need the letter delivered immediately, and I want you to escort Dr. Parker here."

Price nodded. "Of course." He glanced at the envelope. "Dr. Denise Parker. Harvard Stem Cell Institute. Is she in some sort of trouble?"

While he didn't need to explain himself, the Grand Master decided it might drive home the importance of Price's task if he did. "She is meeting her life partners in the introduction ceremony this afternoon, and I'm not sure she'll show up without assistance."

Price frowned. "We don't usually escort members to that ritual. Is she resistant?"

The Grand Master shook his head. "No. She is special."

Price didn't appear satisfied with that response, but he

would soon learn for himself why Denise Parker required the escort. "Very well."

Price turned to leave, but the Grand Master issued one last order.

"Don't leave the facility without Denise, Price. Escort her here. And...for your troubles, you'll find a small reward in box twenty-seven. Make sure you retrieve it as soon as you return."

CHAPTER ONE

Denise Parker lifted her head from the microscope and rubbed her eyes wearily. She'd risen well before dawn after a restless night spent sleeping on the thin cot in her office. Her mother would read her the riot act if she knew how often she stayed at the lab.

Most nights she worked so late she couldn't be bothered driving across town to her tiny apartment. She wasn't married, didn't own pets, hell, she didn't even have plants, so there was very little reason for her to return home. Ever.

She turned to her computer to input the figures and to hash out some ANOVA calculations. Her life seemed to be one long stream of trials and data analysis. Mom despaired over her long hours and disinterest in a social life, but Deni couldn't tell her mother there was no reason to worry. She would definitely get married...someday. She had found a way to guarantee a marriage without the awkwardness of dating.

She'd been introduced to the Trinity Masters just as she was finishing up her doctoral degree. Her professor had asked her to remain after class one day and had opened her eyes to a world she'd never imagined existed—one of secret societies, symbols, ceremonies and power.

As a child prodigy, she'd never fit in anywhere, always years younger than her peers. The Trinity Masters had accepted her despite—no, because of—her intelligence and eccentricities. They supported her endeavors in science, helping her land a job at one of the most respected research labs in the country right after her post-doctorate work. The powerful members had helped pave the way for her controversial research by cutting through red tape and ensuring the continual flow of grant money necessary to allow her to continue her experiments.

She'd overheard some of the single members of the Trinity Masters jokingly refer to their successes as "selling their souls to the devil," but Deni didn't see it that way. Her work would revolutionize modern medicine, enabling doctors to treat and maybe find a cure for Alzheimer's, Parkinson's, ALS and any other neurological disease that crept up. There was too much pain in the world—she had witnessed that firsthand—and she wouldn't rest until she'd done everything in her power to find a way to stop it.

The Trinity Masters's philosophy was based on the belief that there was power in a triad. By binding three intelligent people together, they hoped to strengthen society through relationships formed for a variety of political, scientific and cultural reasons. In exchange for their support on the professional level, the Trinity Masters would place her with two partners who would bind their lives to hers in the ultimate sharing of power and ideas. It was a heady prospect to be part of such an old and elite group.

Deni simply needed to bide her time until the Grand Master called her to the altar. Their concept of an arranged marriage appealed to her because she wasn't willing to sacrifice her research for romance. There was no room in her life for that kind of emotion.

Unfortunately for her relationship with her mother, the Trinity Masters was a secret. Deni wished there was some way she could tell her mother she needn't worry about her only child spending the rest of her life as a spinster. Revealing her life plan would save her countless hours of nagging phone calls and attempts on her mother's part to set her up with some friend's son or the hairdresser's recently divorced nephew.

Oh, well. Until the Grand Master found her suitable partners, she would have to fend off her mother's matchmaking for a few more years. She'd paid close attention to the ages of the recently paired triads. Members were called to the altar between the ages of thirty-two and thirty-seven with an average age for females of thirty-two. Mercifully that meant there was an eighty-four percent likelihood that Deni had at least four more unencumbered years to focus on her research.

She put on a pair of safety goggles and began running the next set of tests. She wasn't sure how long she'd worked—her research assistant, Curtis, always teased her about disappearing into the Twilight Zone during experiments—when the sound of the lab door opening captured her attention.

Glancing up, she found herself face to face with a very large, stern-looking man. The majority of her colleagues had slight builds and pale complexions from too many hours spent inside under the fluorescent lighting. This man with his dark skin, coal-black hair and Mr. Universe-sized muscles was the polar opposite of nearly every man she'd ever met.

With the exception of Gunner. The thought of her only friend made her smile, which produced an even deeper scowl on the stranger's face.

Damn. She had a bad habit of living inside her head and forgetting to communicate.

"What are you doing in here?"

His frown deepened.

Crap. Time to employ social convention. "Hello. Can I help you?"

"Are you Denise Parker?"

She nodded. "Deni."

"Excuse me?"

She wasn't sure why she bothered to correct the man, but she persevered anyway. "Everyone calls me Deni. Never Denise."

The man's expression didn't change. Instead, he extended his hand and offered her a letter. "This is for you, Denise."

She couldn't miss the way he stressed her formal name. Something about the man rubbed her the wrong way. He seemed angry with her, but she couldn't understand why. She'd never met him before.

Deni glanced at the envelope, immediately recognizing the seal of the Trinity Masters. Her heart began to race. There must be a mistake. It was too soon. She was still too young, too busy for this.

She looked at the man again and her hands actually went numb. Surely he wasn't...

No. He couldn't be. She glanced behind him. He was alone. Even so, she felt compelled to make sure. "Shouldn't there be two of you?"

The man's eyes narrowed. "I'm here as the messenger only. Open the letter."

She released a long sigh of relief. "Thank God."

The man glared and she realized she'd spoken aloud. "Um. Sorry."

She tore open the envelope, trying hard to keep him from noticing her suddenly shaking hands. The letter confirmed her fears. She was being summoned.

"Today?" She shook her head. "I can't go today. I have too much to do."

The stranger didn't appear to care if she'd scheduled tea with the Queen of England. With his arms crossed and his legs spread, he reminded her of a bouncer at a nightclub. His stance made it clear she was going, whether she wanted to or not.

"I'm to escort you." He took the letter from her hand and skimmed it quickly. He glanced at his watch. "You're to be there in fifty-five minutes. With traffic, it will take us twenty-five to get to the library. How long will it take you to shut things down here?"

Deni felt a wave of lightheadedness. What the hell was happening? "I need at least fifteen minutes."

He nodded. "Then I suggest you begin."

He walked toward an alcove near the entrance where her research assistant kept his desk. He claimed a chair there and pulled out his phone. He began tapping on it, ignoring her.

Deni glanced down at her wardrobe. She was dressed in faded jeans and a plain black T-shirt, covered by her lab coat. Her hair was haphazardly held in place on top of her head with two pencils she'd relegated to Chinese-hair-stick duty. Even so, she suspected more of it was out of the chignon than in. She didn't dare admit to the man that she'd slept in this outfit last night, too tired to bother undressing before collapsing on the cot. She couldn't show up to meet her prospective partners like this.

"Excuse me, but shouldn't I have received some sort of notice before this?"

The man shrugged. "Did you?"

She shook her head. Then she realized she hadn't been home in three days. "But I've been working around the clock. I haven't been home to get the mail."

"Email?"

Deni crinkled her nose, realizing she'd dug her own grave on this. "I'm not very good about checking that." The last time she had bothered to log in, she'd discovered 417 unread messages. She had logged right off.

"Voice mail?"

She swallowed heavily. "I lost my phone charger a couple of weeks ago. My cell's been dead since then."

"I see now." The man nodded slowly. "You're still going to the ceremony."

Deni wasn't sure what he saw, but it became apparent no force of nature was going to keep this man from delivering her to the library.

She began shutting down the equipment, her mind racing as she tried to think of some way to stall. At least until she could take a shower and put on some clean underwear.

The door to her lab opened again.

"Hey, gorgeous."

Deni smiled, her stress immediately disappearing as Gunner Wells walked in. "Oh my God. Gunner. What are you doing in town?"

Gunner glanced at Mr. Universe in the corner and gave her a funny look. She had no idea how to explain the other man's presence so she decided to dodge the conversation completely.

She stepped around the counter and threw herself into her friend's arms. She'd never needed to see his smiling face more than right now.

Gunner picked her up and spun her around as she laughed. "I've got a meeting and I'm running late. But there was no way I could come to Boston and not see my best girl."

He set her on her feet and gave her a quick up-and-down glance. "You're sleeping in your office again."

She rolled her eyes. Next to her mother, Gunner came a

close second on the nagging routine, determined she needed to leave the lab occasionally and get a life. "I'm working."

"Right. Working." He took a deep breath and Deni knew what was coming next. Gunner didn't disappoint her. "When are you going to get the hell out of here and start living a little, Deni? When's the last time you went on a date? Got laid?"

She blushed, not because of Gunner's questions—they talked openly about everything—but because she was far too aware of the stranger sitting in the corner, listening to their every word. "I don't know. It hasn't been that long."

"Liar." Gunner reached up and ruffled her already messy hair.

She'd met Gunner three years earlier. He was an FBI agent in D.C. and he'd needed to consult a scientific expert for help on a case involving possible biological weapons and national security. A mutual friend had given him her name. After several phone calls and two face-to-face meetings, his case was solved, the country safe. Even so, he continued to call her, and Deni had made her first real friend.

He typically traveled to Boston a few times a year and he never failed to visit her, the two of them meeting for dinner. Her mother had suggested several thousand times Deni should try to change their status from friends to more, but Deni couldn't do that. She couldn't lose the friendship over a more serious relationship that would end the day the Grand Master looked her way.

Her heart lurched at the thought. That day was today.

"So you're here for a meeting?"

Gunner nodded. "Yep. And I'm sorry to say I'm not sure I'll have time for our usual dinner date and catch up. That's why I stopped by now."

There was a sadness in Gunner's eyes Deni wasn't used to

seeing. He was always so cheerful and happy. "Is everything okay?"

"Oh, hell yeah. I'm just busy and bummed we're this close and I can't spend time with you."

She smiled. Gunner didn't mind her workaholic tendencies, her inability to focus on normal conversations for more than five minutes or the fact she'd never seen a single episode of Seinfeld or The Big Bang Theory. She loved the way he would listen to her talk about fibroblasts, DNA, blastocysts and retroviruses for hours on end, all while pretending to understand and be interested.

He was the only person on the planet who'd ever managed to get her to leave the lab at a decent hour and go out to dinner in a restaurant like a normal person. He made her feel pretty and feminine and…sort of warm and fuzzy inside.

She didn't have a clue what it felt like to fall in love. Hell, she'd never even been involved in a romantic relationship. And given the fact she wasn't choosing her future mates, she was fairly certain she'd never know. But part of her thought if she'd ever allowed herself to feel that emotion, Gunner would have been the man to capture her heart.

She recalled the letter from the Grand Master lying on the counter behind her. Her silly dreams about Gunner were completely foolish. She was less than an hour away from meeting her partners. From today forward, there would be two strangers in her life.

The realization of what she'd signed on for terrified her. What if they hated her? Given her present appearance, she was destined to make a terrible first impression.

"Earth to Deni."

She focused on Gunner as he waved his hand in front of her face.

"Sorry."

He grinned and gave her a kiss on the cheek. It was the first time he'd ever shown her that kind of affection. Typically, they kept their physical touches to nothing more than platonic hugs.

"I'm used to you drifting away from me. Maybe one of these days you'll find a way to let me know what's going on inside that busy brain of yours."

She didn't know how to explain that things were going to be different from now on. But until she knew exactly how, she decided to remain silent.

Gunner looked at his watch. "Shit. I have to go, Deni. I wish I had more time this trip, but—"

The stranger by the door cleared his throat, reminding her she was wasting precious time.

"Um, Deni?" Gunner gestured to the man at her assistant's desk with a quick jerk of his head.

"Long story. Tell you later." With any luck, Gunner would forget. Or she'd figure out some lie that would explain the Incredible Hulk's presence in her lab.

"You sure?"

She nodded, touched by his concern. "Everything's okay. I have a meeting in a little while too. Call me when you get back to D.C.?"

"Will do." He grasped her hand and pulled her toward him for one of his big bear hugs. She had to admit, Gunner gave the greatest hugs in the world.

Then, he left her alone with the menacing giant.

"You've managed to waste ten minutes. We need to leave in five."

She turned away before she gave into the juvenile impulse to stick her tongue out at the asshole.

Ten minutes later, she hung her lab coat on the hook by the door and followed the man to the street. Deni caught more than a few of the surprised looks from her colleagues as she said goodbye. She wasn't sure she'd ever left work in the middle of the afternoon. She tried not to think about how today's untimely interruption was putting her behind schedule. She'd just have to make up for it later. Maybe after the ceremony she could come back and pull an all-nighter.

When they exited the building, Deni was surprised to see the stranger walk to a limousine. He opened the door and then gestured for her to enter the vehicle.

Once they were both inside, she looked around, amazed by the elegant space. A long, leather couch spanned one side while a mini-bar occupied the other. They both opted to share the backseat.

Deni was prone to carsickness and considering her stomach was already queasy from nerves, she didn't think she'd better take a risk at not facing forward, even though she'd love to lie down on that long couch just to see if it was as soft as it looked. The limo was almost as big as her apartment.

"I've never been in a limo before. I drive a Smart Car." She looked at the huge man sitting next to her. "Of course, it's probably better we took your car. You wouldn't fit in mine."

He didn't reply. Instead, he stared out the window.

Deni's nervousness grew in the silence. It was clear the man didn't like her, but she could really use a distraction right now. "You know, I just realized, I don't know your name."

The man didn't bother to look at her. "Price."

She considered his answer for a minute and then asked the obvious question. "Is that your first or last name?"

For the first time since he'd entered her lab, the man gave her what she could only assume was his rendition of a smile. Either that or he was fighting a bad case of indigestion. "First."

"Oh. I would have lost that bet. So...you work for the Trinity Masters?"

His scowl returned. "No. I'm a member."

For some odd reason, his answer sent a wave of relief surging through her. "So you've been through this ceremony? You know what's going to happen? I'd feel so much better if you could give me some hint about what my role is. What I'm supposed to do."

Price turned to look at her. "I don't have a clue."

Her shoulders sagged. "You've never been through the introduction ceremony?"

He shook his head. "I'm one of the single members."

His response annoyed her. Price had to be pushing his late thirties. Why was he getting a pass while she was being forced to put her career on hold so early? "How old are you?"

He didn't take offense at her question, though she could tell she surprised him. "I'm thirty-eight. How old are you?"

"Twenty-eight." Great. Price had gotten ten more unencumbered years than she would. How was that fair?

Price studied her face. "You're still quite young."

She nodded. "I thought I had a few more years before I'd be called to the altar."

"You were told at your initiation this call could come at any time."

She shrugged. "I know. And I'm okay with it. I just sort of meant to do a few things before this happened."

Price's face softened and she realized he wasn't quite as fearsome as he'd first appeared. "Like what?"

"Like lose my virginity." She hadn't meant to blurt that out, but her heart was racing a mile a minute, and the closer they got to the library the faster her nervous knee bounced.

Price reached over and used his large hand to still her shaking leg. "You're still a virgin?"

She could feel her face flush, heat permeating her skin. "I don't date much."

"According to your friend, it sounds like you never go out. When was your last date?"

Deni wished she didn't know the answer, but she knew it all too well. "Never."

Price frowned. She couldn't tell if he thought she was lying or pathetic. Both responses sucked.

"Never?"

"I graduated from high school when I was fourteen. Earned my bachelor's degree at seventeen, my masters at nineteen and my doctorate at twenty-two. The majority of my college career was spent in an apartment with my mom."

"I assume you don't still live with your mother."

His tone was the perfect blend of sardonic and serious. She had no idea if he was making fun of her or not, so she gave him the benefit of the doubt. "No. I don't live with my mother anymore."

"Well, congratulations then. Tonight will be a true honeymoon for you. In every sense of the word."

She studied his face, searching for some clue that said he was teasing her. There was nothing there. "Thanks. I guess."

Deni reached into her bag and pulled out her Trinity Masters necklace. She rarely wore the thing as it always seemed to be in her way whenever she worked on experiments in the lab. The only time she ever put it on was for the Trinity Masters' meetings. She slipped it over her head, the expensive gold chain and ornate charm looking out of place against her tatty black T-shirt.

Price nodded approvingly. She glanced at his hand and recognized the Trinity Masters symbol emblazoned on a large gold ring.

She glanced out the window. They were close to the library. During college, that place had been a sanctuary to her. Some people found inner peace in a church. Deni found it at the Boston Public Library. She could walk along the aisles for hours, perusing the shelves, never failing to discover something different, to learn something new.

Now, as the limousine neared Boylston Street, she felt the beginning of true panic. She wasn't ready for this.

"Denise." Price's deep voice captured her attention. She was surprised when he grasped her hand. "Breathe."

She struggled to suck in air, her chest too tight. Great. She was starting to hyperventilate. As if Price didn't have enough reasons to think she was a complete idiot.

"Not like that. Watch me. Match your breathing to mine."

He inhaled slowly, and Deni attempted to follow suit. They exhaled together. Price released a long stream of breath while hers sort of blew out fast and hard. He demonstrated several more times until Deni felt the constriction in her chest ease.

"Better?"

She nodded. "I wish I could've gone home to get a shower."

Price glanced at his watch and gave her a rueful grin. "There really isn't time."

"I know." She pushed a stray piece of hair behind her ear. "How bad do I look?"

Rather than reply, he reached up and released her hair, allowing it to fall over her shoulders. Then he handed her something. "I'd suggest losing the pencils."

She glanced down and laughed as he placed the number twos in her palm. "God. They're going to hate me."

He frowned. "No. I don't think it's possible for anyone to hate you."

Deni bit her lower lip. Though his words were perfectly kind—actually it was one of the nicest compliments she'd ever received—she still couldn't tell if he was sincere. He had a killer poker face. His sweet words didn't seem to match his stern expression. Of course, it didn't help that he was huge and intimidating. She wasn't particularly tall. She purchased most of her clothing in the petite section. Price towered over her.

She turned to watch the people on the street, smiling as a young boy tugged on his mother's hand and pointed to the limo. She glanced at the interior again, wondering what Price did that allowed him to travel in such style. She was tempted to ask for a glass of wine from the mini-bar. Though she didn't normally drink, she thought a couple belts of something alcoholic could only help her present state.

When she combined his size with his scowl, his dark, penetrating gaze, his deep voice and the fact she was trying not to freak out about where they were headed, it occurred to her this limo ride was wasted on her. She wasn't appreciating the luxury.

She started running her fingers through her hair, trying to tame the mass of tangles as much as possible.

"There will be a mirror in the dressing room. You'll have a few minutes to fix yourself up. You remember that you're supposed to undress before donning the robe, right?"

Her mouth fell open. "What?"

Price sighed. "It is customary for the three participants to be introduced and then shed their robes. It symbolizes that you come to your partners with no secrets, nothing to hide. Most keep their underwear on during the introduction, but for the formal binding ceremony a month from now, you will be naked."

Deni grasped her stomach and leaned forward. The sudden alarm on Price's face let her know she looked as bad as she felt. He pressed his hand on the back of her neck, directing her head toward her knees.

"Start breathing again. In through your nose, out from your mouth."

She followed his directions, focusing all her energy on not getting sick. She knew what he said was true. She'd read the fine print when she had signed her name on the dotted line. Unfortunately, she had somehow managed to forget that part. Or had she suppressed it?

She was an only child and a virgin with more than a healthy dose of shyness. Her mind raced to recall if anyone besides her mother had ever seen her naked. Her mother hadn't even seen her without clothes on since she'd hit puberty.

"Denise."

She closed her eyes tightly, trying to ignore the fact the car had stopped.

Price repeated her name. She sat up slowly, trying to find something to focus on. Her gaze landed on Price's face.

"We're here."

She nodded once, unable to respond. Somewhere along the line, her lips had gone numb.

Price ran his hands through her hair, pushing it away from her face. Then, to her surprise, he began fixing it. "You have very pretty hair."

"Thank you."

It was an inane conversation, but somehow Price's strength, his steady hands reassured her.

She could do this. She had to. There was no backing out of the Trinity Masters. Members who did so met with ruin, sometimes even death. She'd heard the stories of those who'd broken the rules, ignored their vows. She'd never failed at anything in her life. Hell, she'd never even gotten a B plus.

Deni felt like a fool for falling apart in front of him. She had become a creature of habit, too ingrained in her daily routine, her work. She had forgotten how to adapt.

"I'm okay now. I can do this."

Price studied her face and then nodded. "Yes. I think you can."

The driver opened the door. Deni grabbed her messenger bag and threw it over her shoulder, surprised when Price got out of the vehicle as well.

"You don't have to walk me in. I know where I'm going." Then she smiled. "I won't run. Promise."

"I've been directed to escort you all the way. That's what I'm going to do."

"Suit yourself." Deni shrugged and headed to the elevator. Neither she nor Price spoke as they rode to the top level. Deni tried to focus all her energy on preparing for what was coming. Inside the rare-books room, she walked directly to the triangle cut into the plaster on the back wall. She ran her finger along the inscription, "Mitimur in Vetitum."

"We strive for the forbidden." She remembered how exciting that had seemed to her in the beginning. She'd been the model child and student all her life. The idea that she might partake in something illicit had spoken to her more than she cared to admit.

She pushed on the triangle and a hidden door slid open. Price followed her into the small closet-like space. She'd never been in the tiny room with another person. It was a tight fit.

Price pointed to the rows of boxes on the wall. "The message said you were to open box forty-one."

She nodded and pushed on the number. Reaching in, she withdrew a note and a key.

You'll find your robe in room B. Right-hand corridor.

Wait until you hear the bell.

Grand Master

She started for the secret elevator, turning back when Price opened a box as well.

"What did you get?"

He narrowed his eyes at her nosiness. "None of your business." He placed an envelope in the pocket of his jacket and gestured for her to keep moving.

The second elevator wasn't open to the general public. In fact, she'd venture to guess there were very few library employees who even knew of its existence.

When the doors opened, she stepped out. She'd walked along these hallways many times in the past, but she'd never traveled down the right corridor. The left led to the group dressing rooms, fancy spa-like accommodations where members could put on their robes before ceremonies.

She turned down the unfamiliar hallway and stopped outside room B. "I guess this is me."

"Good luck, Denise."

She gave him an appreciative smile. In his own gruff way, he had helped her today, kept her somewhat calm, gotten her here in one piece. "Thanks for the ride, Price."

He nodded once and then walked away.

Deni took a deep breath and entered the dressing room.

My future starts today.

CHAPTER TWO

Price walked away from Denise feeling equal parts relieved to be rid of her and worried that he should go back to make sure she was okay. He now understood the Grand Master's insistence that she be escorted to the ceremony. The woman was unlike any Trinity Master he'd ever met.

Their society was one of intelligent, self-assured, powerful people. Though obviously brilliant, given her fast track through the educational system, Denise didn't fit any of the other molds. She was unorganized, nervous and inexperienced. His head was still reeling over her virginity confession. Her partners would have their hands full with her. Fortunately for him, his association with Denise Parker was concluded.

Price reached into his pocket and pulled out his so-called reward. He grinned. After the afternoon he'd just endured, the Grand Master better have sprung for passes to scuba dive in protected waters.

Reaching inside, he discovered a letter. One very similar to the message he'd just delivered to...

No. Fuck, no.

Price crumpled up the sheet of paper and shook his head. This was a joke. It had to be.

Glancing down the corridor, he waited. For what? For someone to jump out and yell gotcha?

The hallway was eerily quiet. He opened his fist and looked at the note once more.

You'll find your robe in room A. Right-hand corridor.

Wait until you hear the bell.

Grand Master

That was it? He'd offered nearly a decade of friendship to the Grand Master only to receive this summons. No warning. No consideration of what Price might want from his prospective partners. Jesus. He sure as hell didn't want Denise Parker.

The tiny woman was a mess.

Price looked at his watch. He had five minutes until the bell would ring. Five minutes until his life went off-track. The Grand Master had timed it this way on purpose. He'd known Price would attempt to find a way out of this partnership if given the time. Now...

He walked slowly toward room A, recalling his conversation with the Grand Master this morning. Price had pledged his loyalty to the Trinity Masters and to their leader.

This rule was absolute. Members were placed in threesomes and the commitment to that triad was unbreakable. Permanent. Even so, Price struggled to understand what benefit to society could sprout from a marriage between him and the tiny scientist. Their lives, their skill sets were as different as mud and chocolate. This didn't make sense.

He sighed. The Grand Master had commanded him to be here, and Price had no choice but to obey. To leave would be tantamount to signing his own death warrant. He swallowed his pride as he stood outside the dressing room. Glancing down the hall, he only had a moment to think, "who's behind door C?" before he entered and began to undress.

The bell rang just as Price pulled up the hood of his black robe. He walked into the ceremony room, resentment growing with every step. The walls of the room were cast in shadows, the lighting focused on the bronze medallion of the Trinity Masters' symbol set into the floor. Three chairs surrounded the circle.

Price watched Denise emerge somewhat timidly from her dressing room, dressed in a long white robe. Then a third person, a man, given the black robe, appeared.

Price's anger returned full-force. He'd been partnered with Denise and another man. He clenched his fists, fighting the instinct to find where the Grand Master stood in the shadows and beat the shit out of the man. He'd expected the introduction ceremony to be one of the best days of his life.

Now, he felt like a man facing his execution, waiting for the hoods to drop and the noose to tighten around his neck.

They each took their seats as the Grand Master appeared. Though Price's face was hidden beneath the hood, he kept his eyes on his leader, willing his so-called friend to understand what he thought of this betrayal.

The Grand Master raised his hands. "Welcome."

Denise and the other man replied with a reverent, "Grand Master," but Price remained silent.

"When you joined the Trinity Masters, you made a vow. You pledged your lives to our cause and our traditions. The time has come for you to meet your partners, your lovers, your spouses. When I call your name, stand and remove your robe."

Price looked toward Denise, understanding exactly how much she dreaded this part. How would she feel when she realized he was one of the men with her? He had sensed she was just a bit afraid of him, and he'd done precious little to alleviate that fear.

"Denise Parker." The Grand Master went straight for the jugular, forcing Denise to go first. Price was tempted to rise and throw off his robe first, in hopes of making it easier for her. To do so was to invite disaster. The Grand Master didn't forgive slights, no matter how small.

Denise stood and pulled down her hood. There was a sharp inhalation from the other man, so Price turned his attention to the one unknown in the room. From his reaction, Price couldn't tell if the man was horrified or captivated by Denise. While she wasn't what Price would call a raving beauty, Denise was definitely pretty. She appeared to have found a brush and some makeup in the dressing room, as her long blonde hair now lay soft against her shoulders, the tangles tamed. She'd also outlined her eyes, drawing his attention to them for the first time. They were the brightest blue he'd ever seen. Maybe he'd been wrong. Without her safety goggles and the pencils in her hair, his tiny scientist was beautiful.

His.

God. Had he already begun to accept she belonged to him?

Denise's hands shook uncontrollably as she tackled the hooks on her robe. Price was about to help her when the Grand Master reached out. He grasped her hand and gave it a slight squeeze. Price heard him whisper, "It's okay," before releasing her once more to finish her task. Once the robe was unfastened, Denise stiffened her shoulders and pulled the material away.

Fuck him.

The lab coat and baggy T-shirt had hidden far too much. His first order of business would be to buy his new wife clothing that accentuated her sexy figure. Even in her plain cotton panties and bra, she was breathtaking. He'd always considered himself a leg man, but Denise's hourglass shape, her large breasts and wide hips had him reconsidering that position. A man could lose himself forever in her luscious curves.

Before his lustful thoughts could take root, the Grand Master spoke again.

"Price Bennett."

He heard Denise whisper, "No," as he rose. He threw off his hood and robe, his anger returning as he glared at the Grand Master. If he'd understood what his true role today was, he would have tried to make a better impression, ease Denise into the situation. As it was, the Grand Master had put him at a distinct disadvantage.

God. He had no business being here. Denise's response proved that.

Standing in his boxers, he crossed his arms, refusing to look at his partners.

"Gunner Wells."

The name rang a bell and curiosity won out as Price watched the other man disrobe. It was the man from the lab, Denise's friend. From the corner of his eye, he watched Denise's face evolve from surprise to sheer delight.

Gunner stood before them in black boxer briefs, a perfect specimen of a man. He had what Price called a pretty-boy face, light-brown hair that hung longer on top, green eyes and a clean-shave. While Price employed weightlifting to increase his muscle mass, Gunner appeared to maintain his trim build with cardio. He had a runner's body.

Gunner caught him staring and offered him a friendly, harmless smile before he turned back to look at Denise with nothing short of pure joy in his face.

Great. The Grand Master had slammed him into a threesome with two people who already knew each other and would be perfectly content to live happily ever after as a couple. Where did that leave him?

The Grand Master had an answer for that too. "You now belong to one another. Come forward."

All of them reached out with their right hands as the Grand Master removed the heavy gold chain from his neck. He wrapped it around their wrists, binding them together. They'd passed the point of no return. From this moment forward, Price's life would be entwined with these two people. In a matter of minutes, they had become his future.

Gunner was the first to move. He leaned forward and pressed a soft, quick kiss on Denise's lips. A slight flush colored her cheeks. She looked like a young girl with her first love. Shit. For all Price knew, Gunner had just given Denise her first kiss. That thought stuck in his craw.

If it was her first kiss, Price was going to make damn sure it was the second she remembered. When Gunner and Denise parted, Price was there. He cupped her cheek with his free hand. He wasn't interested in nice and easy. That had never been his way. He pressed his mouth to hers, firmly using his grip on her face to hold her still. Then he nipped her lower lip, taking advantage when she opened her mouth and gasped. Using his tongue, he explored the wet, sweet warmth. He was surprised—and aroused—when Denise returned the touch, brushing her tongue against his.

He wasn't sure how long they stood there, learning each other's tastes and smells, but Price recalled they weren't alone when the Grand Master cleared his throat. Price released her, pleased to see her face wasn't merely pink, but bright red. He looked at Gunner, expecting to receive a look of disdain, of rebuke. What he didn't anticipate was to find Gunner studying Denise's face curiously.

"Your relationship is yours. You will choose how to live your lives, but there are rules. No one must know about the trinity and you may never stray outside your marriage." The

Grand Master removed the chain from their wrists. "You have one month to get your affairs in order. At that time, you will return here and be formally bound in the marriage of the Trinity Masters. Now go."

The Grand Master left without a backwards glance, which irritated Price. Denise bent over to retrieve her robe and quickly put it back on.

Nothing like spending your honeymoon with a shy, innocent bride and a stranger. Price's anger returned.

"My limo is still outside. I suspect when we return to the dressing rooms we'll discover keycards to a hotel suite. We can travel there together if you'd like."

Gunner nodded. "Sounds good to me. I arrived here by taxi and my suitcase is in the dressing room."

"Good. I can have my driver pick up spare clothes for me once he's dropped us off." Price looked at Denise. "We can swing by your apartment for clothing. Unless you'd prefer to spend yet another night in the same jeans and T-shirt."

She narrowed her eyes. "You said it wasn't you. That you weren't—"

"I didn't know I would be participating in this ceremony until I opened that letter."

Denise bit her lower lip anxiously. "Oh." She gave him a contrite grin. "Sorry."

Price wasn't sure if she was apologizing for her accusation or the marriage. It didn't matter either way. She'd already turned her attention to Gunner.

"I didn't know you were a member of the Trinity Masters," she said.

Gunner smiled. "How could you? It's a secret. We wear masks at social events, and I'm afraid I don't attend as many of those as I'd like. Work usually interferes." Gunner ran his knuckles along her cheek.

Denise grasped Gunner's hand as he started to pull it back. She looked at his Trinity Masters' ring. "I've never seen you wear this."

Gunner shrugged. "In my line of work, it's best not to wear anything too distinguishable." Gunner lifted the charm on her necklace. "I could say the same thing about this."

Denise grinned. "It was always getting caught on stuff in the lab. I broke the chain twice before I finally just put it away. I only wear it to Trinity Masters' get-togethers."

"That makes sense. I suppose I should have suspected you were a member. When I was looking for a scientist with the knowledge to help me with my case a few years back, I went to my old biology professor. He's part of the Trinity Masters, and he directed me to you."

"Professor Moreau. He's the one who introduced me to the Trinity Masters."

Price didn't like being reminded of Denise and Gunner's long history. "If you two are finished with your walk down memory lane, I'd like to leave."

He wanted to kick himself when Denise's smile faded, her gaze turning leery as she looked at him. "Okay. You know if you want to, you could just have your driver drop me off at the lab. I can get my car, head to my apartment to pack and meet you both at the hotel later."

Gunner chuckled. "No dice. I know you. You'll pop into the lab to check one little thing and we won't see you again for six months. We're sticking...like glue."

Price appreciated Gunner's help. He'd opened his mouth to say, "hell no," but the other man's response had been worded in such a way that Denise didn't become irritated. Until some of her fear of him abated, Price was going to have to tread lightly, an act that didn't come naturally.

"Fine. But I definitely need to go back to work tomorrow."

Gunner's gaze met his and Price felt an odd connection to the man. Almost as if he could read his thoughts. Gunner knew as well as he did that Denise wouldn't be returning to work tomorrow. Or even the next day. The three of them had too much to sort out, lives to connect, living situations to arrange, and...sex.

Price had participated in ménages before, with two women and sometimes with a woman and another man. He was no stranger to the logistics. It would take them time to ease Denise into exactly what the consequences of this arrangement would mean for her. She obviously hadn't put together the fact she was the only woman bound in marriage to two straight men.

Price put his hand on her back. "We'll see," was all he said in response to her assertion she'd return to work. Better to save that argument for another day. Tonight was going to be difficult enough.

Each of them returned to their private rooms to get dressed and gather their things. Then they met up in the corridor a few minutes later and walked to the limousine in silence.

Price didn't miss the way Gunner placed his hand on the small of Denise's back in a familiar, friendly way. She didn't shirk from the other man's touch. In fact, she leaned toward him, encouraging Gunner to pull her closer. Price rubbed his temple, fighting against the growing pressure. If he didn't find a way to calm down, he'd spend the evening with a killer migraine.

He closed his eyes once they were all seated in the car. He'd studied Aikido for several years and, while he'd long since moved on to learn other forms of martial arts, he still employed the relaxation techniques as a way of centering himself.

Mercifully, Denise and Gunner seemed to need some time for quiet reflection as well. The trip to Denise's apartment was made in complete silence.

When they arrived, Price felt calmer. Denise opened the door before his driver, Roman, could get there.

She apologized when Roman jogged around the car to offer her his hand. "Oh, oops. I was supposed to wait, wasn't I? Sorry."

Roman smiled. "No problem, Miss."

He and Gunner followed her out.

Denise frowned. "I'll only be a minute. You guys can wait here."

Gunner grasped her hand and led her to the front entrance of her building. "Nope. I'm coming up. I've always wanted to see what your place looks like. In my mind, I'm picturing every surface covered in test tubes, boiling brews and microscopes, as well as a half-completed Frankenstein lying on your dining room table. Am I close?"

Deni laughed. "Busted. Don't touch the monster though or he might come to life." She raised her hands in what Price assumed was supposed to be a threatening pose.

He followed them in silence, trying not to lose the composure he'd just managed to regain in the car. However, it was difficult given their surroundings. There was no way in hell Denise was keeping this place after they were formally bound. He'd been surprised when she'd given her address to Roman. Surely she made enough money at the lab that she didn't have to live in such a shady neighborhood. Plus, the security in her building was deplorable. Anyone could walk in from the street and roam the dimly lit hallways.

Denise led them to the second floor, but she stopped short when they reached her apartment.

"What's wrong?" Gunner asked.

"The door's ajar."

Price's instincts took over. He stepped around Denise and pushed her behind him. He noticed Gunner's response mirrored his. Both of them reached for their backs and produced guns. Interesting. He was going to have to find out what Gunner Wells did for a living.

"You have guns? Both of you?"

Price shushed Denise, pushing her more securely behind him when she moved toward the door. "Quiet."

Denise obeyed, then he felt her hands close around the material of his shirt. He tried to ignore how much he liked that she trusted him to protect her. She wasn't shirking away from him, rather she was moving closer.

Gunner stood to the side, gun at the ready as Price slowly pushed the door open. The apartment was destroyed, furniture overturned, dishes and picture frames shattered, books and papers covered the floor.

Denise gave a small sound of distress, clinging tighter as they slowly entered the room. Gunner quietly and efficiently walked down the hallway, peering into the other rooms while Price kept Denise covered.

"No one's here," Gunner said, sliding his gun back into his waistband.

Price turned, struggling to pull Denise's hands from his shirt. She was pale, trembling.

"My stuff."

It was demolished. Her TV had been kicked in, her couch cushions shredded. Price wasn't sure he'd ever seen such a malicious attack on a place. This wasn't a robbery. It was destruction.

Gunner looked miserable as he gestured down the corridor. "There's something you should look at in the bedroom."

Price put a supportive arm around her waist as they walked toward her room. Though she was visibly shaken, she was holding up better than Price expected.

Denise released a long, shaky breath as they stood at the doorway. "Shit."

Above her bed, someone had painted the words Baby Killer in bright red. The paint was thick enough that it ran along the walls and dripped onto the bed, looking far too much like blood.

"Assholes. How many times do I have to explain what I do? People are so stupid."

Price admired the spunkiness in her voice. While most women would have been terrified by such a horrifying message, it appeared to fuel Denise's anger. Maybe he'd misread his absent-minded, hyperventilating virgin scientist. There was spirit in her.

She started to step into the room but something caught Price's eye. He grasped her waist and pulled her back, jerking her hard against his chest.

"Price. It's okay. It's just paint."

"Don't move." He pushed Denise toward Gunner, who remained in the hallway, then he dropped to his knees. "Tripwire."

"No fucking way," Gunner said.

"What's that mean?" Denise asked.

Price followed the wire, careful not to touch it. It disappeared under an overturned laundry basket. He ventured a guess they'd find an explosive device hidden there.

"What do you do for a living, Gunner?" he asked.

"FBI."

Price nodded. "Good. Call the Boston office. Get them to send a bomb squad over here. Denise, you're getting the fuck out of here."

"Hating what I do is one thing, but wanting to blow me up is just stupid. How did they plant a bomb in my house?"

Price rose and took her arm. "I have no idea, but until we

figure it out, you've just bought yourself two permanent shadows."

Gunner followed them downstairs, describing to someone on the other end of his cell what they'd discovered. In the meantime, Price found the landlord's apartment and informed the man he needed to evacuate the building. Through it all, Denise remained silent, though Price was happy to see her color had returned.

In fact, she seemed extremely composed. Price didn't know what to make of a woman who took a bomb in her apartment in stride while having a full-blown panic attack over standing in front of two men in her underwear. She was a puzzle, an enigma, an unexpected surprise.

Once they had alerted the landlord and Gunner had called in the cavalry, they escorted Denise back to the limo. Price got in, expecting her to follow, but she remained behind.

"Aren't you coming?" she asked Gunner.

Gunner shook his head. "No. I'm going to wait here for the bomb squad. One of my friends in the Boston office is coming as well. He's going to open an investigation and I need to give him some information. I suspect he'll want to talk to you as well, but I'll hold him off until tomorrow."

Price appreciated Gunner's consideration. He could see Denise did too.

Gunner grasped her hand and kissed her palm. Price expected some of the jealousy he'd experienced during the ceremony to return, but it didn't. Instead, he felt a spark of arousal at the sight of Gunner touching their woman.

Interesting.

"We're going to put all of this behind us tonight. Focus on the positive stuff that happened today," Gunner promised her.

Denise looked down, her confidence fading. "You think this is positive? The three of us?"

Gunner grinned. "Hell yeah. Don't you?"

She shrugged and glanced toward the open door of the car. Price had placed himself far enough away that he was hidden in the shadows but still able to see her. "I guess so. I mean—" she lowered her voice and Price found himself bending forward to hear, "—I don't think Price is attracted to me. You know, that way. I was wondering if..."

Her words drifted away, but he'd heard enough. They went through him like a knife.

"You want to know if I'm sexually attracted to you?" Gunner asked.

Denise nodded.

"I want you so bad it hurts." Gunner took their still-linked hands and rubbed her fingers along his chest. "Soon I'll show you exactly how much."

Deni's eyes widened. "I'm scared," she whispered.

Gunner kissed her, that same sweet meeting of lips they'd shared back at the library. Price knew he'd never be able to offer her the same. His desire for her had risen to ridiculous levels, his cock so hard he feared he'd split the seam in his dress pants. What he felt for the little innocent was far from tame. It was primal, wild, ready to be unleashed.

He'd show Denise Parker exactly how attracted he was to her.

"Go to the hotel with Price and take a nice long, hot shower. When I get there, we'll order room service and start figuring things out. Okay?"

Denise nodded and then climbed into the car. Gunner leaned forward, his gaze capturing Price's.

"Don't start without me, you two." Though his words were spoken in an easy, friendly tone, Price didn't miss the warning on the man's face.

"We're a threesome," Price said, issuing his own reminder. "Remember?"

Gunner nodded once and then shut the door.

Denise turned to look out the window, but Price wasn't willing to give her any space. He moved, claiming the spot next to her.

"Denise."

"My name is Deni."

For some reason, he couldn't call her that, couldn't picture her as anything other than Denise. "I know."

"But you're still not going to use that name, are you?"

He shook his head. "No. Deni is a girl's name. You aren't a little girl. You're a woman. My woman."

"That sounds ridiculously caveman-like."

Price grinned. "Maybe so, but I take care of what's mine."

She bit her lower lip, a nervous gesture Price was beginning to find endearing. He reached up and tugged on her chin, forcing her to stop.

"Don't hurt those lips. I intend to spend hours kissing them later."

She blinked rapidly. "But I thought—"

"I heard what you thought. You're wrong. I'm very attracted to you, Denise. Do you want proof?"

Her gaze drifted to his pants. He didn't bother to cover the obvious erection pressing against the fabric. When she realized where she was looking, her gaze snapped back to his face.

"You understand what's going to happen tonight?"

She nodded. "We're going to have sex."

"All three of us. Do you masturbate?"

Her face flushed. "What?"

"It's a simple enough question."

"Why do you want to know?"

He leaned closer, letting her adjust to his nearness. This

time, she didn't flinch or move away. Progress. "I need to know exactly what your past experiences have involved. You've never had intercourse with a man, but what about foreplay?"

She pressed her eyes closed tightly and looked away. "No one's ever touched me. Down there."

"Yourself included?"

She didn't open her eyes. "I have."

"How?"

She released a long breath but didn't reply.

Price cupped her cheek, forced her to face him. "Open your eyes, Denise. There will be no secrets between us. Not anymore. How do you touch yourself?"

"I rub my clit."

"And?"

"I use my fingers."

"How many?"

She pushed his hand away from her face. "God, does this really matter?"

He didn't respond. Instead, he waited, holding her gaze.

"I don't know. Two, three?"

"What about toys? Dildos. Vibrators."

"I don't own any. When I feel horny, I just use my fingers, rub myself until I..."

"Come?"

She nodded. "Sometimes. Sometimes the feeling just sort of goes away and I stop."

"The feeling stops?"

She blushed and lifted one shoulder in response.

"I'll make sure it never goes away again." Over the course of the afternoon, Price had run the gamut of emotions. From annoyance to wounded pride, confusion to anger. Now he was overwhelmed by this...this unexplainable need to stake an irrefutable claim on Denise Parker. He'd known her less than a few hours and yet the connection was there, growing stronger by the minute.

The idea that Gunner would be there as well somehow sweetened the pot. Price had always known he'd found his niche, his place in life. The Trinity Masters fit him like a glove, their philosophies, their lifestyle. Everything.

"You belong to us now, Denise. Gunner and I will take care of those needs for you."

"Can I ask a question?"

He grinned. "Of course."

"How does it work with three of us? Will you just take turns? Or…"

"Or?"

She shook her head. "You're the one with all the answers. Just tell me."

Her expression told him she knew what his response would be. Even so, he'd just promised they wouldn't have secrets. "Tonight, I suspect we'll take turns as you said. You're new to this and neither of us wants to hurt or scare you."

"But," she prompted.

"Eventually, we will expand on your experience."

"How?" Her voice was growing stronger with each question, her curiosity stronger than her reticence.

He liked her best when she was in the mood to challenge him. "We're going to fuck your ass and your mouth and I have every intention of putting my cock between those pretty tits of yours and—"

"Got it." She raised her hand. "I don't need to hear anything else."

"Are you okay with that?"

"Do I have a choice?"

He frowned. "You will always have a choice."

She seemed genuinely surprised by his response. "Oh. Well, I think I'd like to try that."

"Which part?"

She looked away as she said, "All of it."

He chuckled. "Good. But I think we'd better change the subject or I'm going to forget all about Gunner and take you right here in the limo."

She gave him a wicked grin. "Probably not a good idea to piss off a man with a gun."

Price placed his arm along the backseat, stroking her hair. "I'm not worried. Mine's bigger."

"Overcompensating for something?"

He tugged on her hair and laughed. "You're a minx. And you're only baiting the bear. New topic. Who do you think did that to your apartment?"

Denise sobered up and shrugged. "I have no idea."

"It didn't seem like that earlier. When we discovered the paint on the wall, you called them assholes. It sounded like you suspected someone."

"I gave a speech a few months ago at the library about the importance of stem-cell research. We were trying to raise funds for a new project we're working on. Grant money has been harder and harder to come by in this economy. There were some protestors there. They caused a ruckus and the police even arrested their leader, some scary-looking dude they all called the Reverend, although if he's ordained in any legitimate church, I'd be seriously shocked."

"What was their protest based on?"

"The same old controversy that always surrounds my research. There are a lot of people who disagree with scientists using human embryos. But if the idiot had listened to my speech instead of climbing on his soapbox and spouting inanities, he would have heard me say we rarely use human tissue at the institute as it's very hard to get. Most of my work is done with Mus musculus."

Price tilted his head and she laughed.

"Sorry. Fancy name for mice. In the mouse cell we only use trophoblastic cells, which are the cells that eventually become the chorion, the embryonic placenta. They are the inner mass cells, which actually become the embryo we leave alone. We believe—"

Price held up his hand to stop her. "Let's cut to the chase. Do you think this Reverend guy could be behind the break-in?"

She shook her head. "I'm afraid he's just one of many who aren't fond of my work. I can't really point the finger at him specifically. I mean, we've been getting some pretty nasty phone calls lately at the lab, but the voice is always female, so that's obviously not the Reverend. Then someone keyed the door of my car. I've been driving around town for two weeks with the word Satan scratched in the paint. I haven't had time to take it to the shop to get it fixed."

Price's temper flared as she described the attacks. "Did you report any of this to the police?"

She lifted one shoulder, casually dismissing the danger. "No. I've been busy and none of it was that terrible. Until tonight." Her voice broke a little on the last word. Price was almost relieved to spy that slightest bit of emotion on her part. She'd been too calm since they'd left her apartment.

"I'm sure your insurance policy will cover the damages. Besides, you may not need to replace it all. My house is fully furnished."

She frowned. "So?"

Price didn't have time to answer as the limousine pulled up in front of the hotel. "We'll finish this discussion when Gunner arrives."

Roman opened the door and Price helped Denise out of the

car. He held her hand, marveling at the difference a few hours could bring. He'd begun the day a footloose, fancy-free bachelor, and then spent the majority of his afternoon pissed as shit. Tonight, he would fall asleep with his virgin bride and an FBI agent. He chuckled to himself.

Life had just become intriguing.

CHAPTER THREE

Gunner stood outside the door to the hotel suite, staring at the keycard in his hand. Nothing about today had turned out the way he had expected. And yet, he couldn't imagine a better outcome. He'd had a thing for Deni Parker since the first day they'd met. Unfortunately, geography and the Trinity Masters had kept him from pursuing her. He knew he'd never be satisfied with a long-distance relationship and he never doubted he would fall in love with her. Because of his membership in the Trinity Masters, he'd held back, unwilling to risk her heart—and his—on something that couldn't last.

He pressed his head against the cool wood of the door and grinned. Deni was part of the Trinity Masters. She was the last person on earth he would have pegged as a member, but now that he thought about it, it made sense. There was no denying she was brilliant. Beneath her wrinkled clothing, wholesome face and endearing shyness lurked an intelligent mind and a kind heart. That combination had been deadly to his libido for years.

Now she was his. They'd pledged to spend their lives together.

With Price.

Price Bennett was the reason Gunner wasn't throwing open the hotel door and rushing straight into Deni's arms. The man was a crouching tiger in a two-thousand dollar custom-made suit. He was the unknown variable. And after nearly a decade with the FBI, Gunner had come to hate indefinites. It was his job to uncover secrets, expose lies, and he was determined to figure Price out.

The problem was time. He didn't have any. Once he entered the hotel room, for better or worse, he was going to have to put his trust in a man he didn't know. And that was something he'd never done before. While waiting for the bomb squad to disarm the device in Deni's apartment, Gunner had run a background check on Price.

He had to admit what he'd discovered about the man professionally impressed him. Price was the CEO and owner of one of top—if not the best—international security companies in the world. He had offices in Boston, New York, London, Istanbul and Hong Kong and his employees had protected everyone from princes to rock stars to ambassadors.

The success of his Fortune 500 company, along with a pile of old family money, had landed Price a spot on the list of the world's most eligible billionaires for three years running.

Needless to say, the man had a reputation as a lady-killer. He'd been romantically linked to two movie stars, a fashion model and the reigning queen of Billboard's Top 40 list.

While the three of them were supposed to be partners, not adversaries, Gunner suspected battle lines would be drawn quickly if Price did anything to hurt Deni. He'd spotted the man sitting in her office earlier, prior to the ceremony. Now he understood what Deni meant by a long story.

Given Deni's shocked response when Price removed his hood, she hadn't been expecting—or thrilled—by the match. In fact, until discovering the break-in at her apartment, Gunner had gotten a sense Deni was afraid of Price.

He didn't blame her. He was well aware of Deni's inexperience with men. Price seemed to be ten men rolled into one. And while Price would be hard enough for Deni to handle on her own, she didn't have just him to contend with. She had Gunner as well. As much as he wanted to take tonight slow, to offer Deni the magic and romance she deserved, he feared he didn't have it in him. Price's presence was a challenge. He had wanted to be the one at the ceremony grasping Deni's face and giving her that hard, open-mouthed kiss he guaranteed she'd never forget.

He wasn't an easy lover. He'd never played that role, but Deni would likely cast him in it because to her he was easygoing, friendly, harmless Gunner. Somehow he had to open her eyes to the real Gunner, reveal the true man without frightening her or losing her trust.

Gunner straightened. There was only one path to walk. And it was through this door.

He entered the suite. It was incredibly elegant, luxurious. Price stood behind a bar, pouring a drink while Deni sat on a plush loveseat. She'd obviously showered, her long blonde hair still damp and neatly brushed back. She appeared to be wearing one of Price's company T-shirts, the Bennett Security logo emblazoned on it. It was ridiculously large and hung to her knees. Clearly even that wasn't enough material for Deni as she continued to tug it lower. Without makeup and her hair hanging loose, she looked incredibly young. Her shyness was going to present a very big obstacle for them.

He nodded once when Price silently lifted a bottle of

whiskey and pointed to him. He watched as the other man poured out two shots. He could use a belt. Or three.

Deni had already helped herself to a drink. A half-full wineglass sat on the side table next to her.

"Was it a bomb?" she asked.

He crossed the room and sank down next to her. "I'm afraid so. It's been disarmed. My friend at the FBI took it back to the office to study. Maybe the design will trigger an MO, give us a suspect. He wants to question you tomorrow morning." Gunner looked at Price. "I'm going to ask him to come here. I suspect this place is secure enough. I'd rather not risk taking Deni out in the open until we determine exactly how serious this threat is."

Price claimed the chair across from them. "I'd say a bomb makes it pretty damn serious, but I agree. It's too dangerous to take her out in the open. The man can come here to talk to her."

Deni leaned forward, piercing them both with her glare. "Oh, I'm sorry. When did I leave the room?"

Gunner grinned. Deni was equal parts sweet and sassy. "Deni," he started.

Price scowled. "It doesn't matter if you're in the room or not, Denise. Gunner and I are going to keep you safe. Given the fact we're both trained professionals in security, and you're not, it makes sense for us to make the arrangements."

"Not when it's my life you're talking about. I told you earlier, I have to go back to work tomorrow."

Price shook his head. "That's not going to happen."

Deni stood up. The T-shirt stopped just shy of her knees, giving Gunner a clear view of her trim calves. The woman lived in jeans, and it occurred to him he'd never seen her in a skirt. They'd have to buy her some. She had beautiful legs.

Walking around the coffee table, Deni planted herself

directly in front of Price. She was pissed. "I've had it up to here with your proclamations. I don't know who the hell you think you are, but no one tells me what to do. I may be young and I may not know a lot of stuff about sex and shit like that, but that doesn't mean I can't take care of myself."

She was furious and waving her arms about, making her agitation obvious. The day's events were clearly catching up to her. Deni tried to be a fighter, but she wasn't particularly good at it. Gunner turned his head, lest she catch him grinning at her flustered attempts at asserting her authority. Maybe he didn't have to worry about Price after all. Deni, in her cute, clumsy way, was handling the man just fine. "I'm perfectly capable of organizing my own affairs," she added.

To his credit, Price let her have her say, keeping his seat rather than standing and stealing the power position away from her. "Are you really? Dead cell phone? Driving a scratched-up car? Not bothering to check your email? These are considered good organizational skills?"

Deni put her hands on her hips. "I'm serious about my job. Those other things don't matter."

Price grinned. "So the only thing you need help with is the sex-and-shit-like-that stuff?"

She shot him a dirty look. "You know what I mean. If you insist on calling me Denise and feeding me that line about me being a woman, not a girl, then you're going to have to toe the line and treat me like an adult. Otherwise, you might as well just call me Deni."

"Fine, Denise. Let's have a rational, adult conversation, shall we?"

His calm response took some of the wind out of Deni's sails.

"My research is very important to me and I've been making

some real progress lately. I can't lose my momentum. It's taken me years to get to this point."

Gunner knew that, understood her concerns. Deni was married to her work. It was going to take time for her to adjust to what he hoped their life would become. "We know that, Deni. We'd never belittle what you do or fail to acknowledge how valuable it is. But, gorgeous, you've given your life to that research, to the lab, and now your life is at risk. Until the threat against you is removed, keeping you safe is our top priority. Then...after that danger is removed, we're going to have to figure out how to make this relationship work. I suspect it will mean sacrifices on all of our parts."

Deni sank down onto the coffee table. "What do you mean?"

Price took a sip of his whiskey. "He means you're not going to sleep at the lab anymore. You'll be in bed—with us—every night."

"I don't think I can make that promise."

Deni wasn't being purposely stubborn, Gunner could see that. In fact, she appeared to be panicking. He rose, kneeling in front of her. "Why don't we tackle some of the easier things first?"

Before he could steer the conversation to safer waters, there was a knock at the door.

"That will be room service." Price rose to answer. "Deni ordered something for you, Gunner. Claimed it was your favorite."

Gunner grinned. "Bacon cheeseburger?"

She laughed. "Yep. Congestive heart failure on a sesame-seed bun with a side of artery-clogging fries."

Gunner took her hand and led her to a small dining table in the corner. He was accustomed to her making fun of his poor diet choices. Typically, he ate healthy meals at home, but whenever they went out for dinner, he splurged. "Extra pickles?"

"Is there any other way?"

Price signed the slip, tipped the waiter and carried the tray over. They were quiet as each of them claimed their meals, some silverware and Price refilled their drinks.

They discussed insignificant things as they ate—the weather in Boston, the strength of the Celtics bench in a recent game, which movie they thought should win the Oscar. It was a surprisingly easy meal when Gunner considered he was sitting with the two people—one a complete stranger—he'd just vowed to spend his life with.

After dinner, they returned to the comfortable seats in the living area. Price reclaimed his earlier chair while Gunner shared the loveseat with Deni again. Her hair had long since dried, natural waves curling around her pretty face. He found it difficult to look at her without imagining gripping those soft tresses as he pressed his cock deep inside her. He shifted, trying to keep his erection at bay. It was getting more difficult as the evening gave way to night. The moment of truth loomed ever nearer.

Time to get serious. He placed his arm along the back of the couch, enjoying the way Deni moved closer. "So, I suppose we need to figure some things out. Should we knock them down? One at a time?"

"Fire away," Price said.

Gunner started with an easy one. "Living situation."

"Denise's house is trashed, and I'm not happy with the neighborhood. It's unsafe. Since she and I both live and work in Boston, I'd like to offer my home as an option."

Gunner could just imagine the opulence of Price's house. This was a man whose primary form of transportation was a limousine with a personal driver. "I could request a transfer to the Boston office, but I'm not sure how quickly something like that could be processed."

Price raised an eyebrow. "With the Trinity Masters' influence? I suspect we could make it happen faster than you think."

Gunner didn't reply, puzzling over Price's use of the word we. Price seemed to have an inside track to the internal workings of the Trinity Masters that he certainly didn't possess.

They both turned to Deni.

"I don't really have a place to go right now. My apartment is destroyed and you've ruled out the cot in my lab as a viable option."

Gunner's chest tightened at the unhappiness on her face. He'd never seen his little spitfire scientist looking so lost. She'd spent the majority of her life alone, without friends or lovers. She truly had no idea how to fit into a real relationship. "Deni. We'll all make a home together. There are three of us now. You don't have to worry about anything."

"Gunner's right. We have time to sort this out, find answers we're all comfortable with."

Deni nodded. "What do you do for a living, Price?"

Gunner realized that while he'd cheated, Deni was still flying blind in regards to Price Bennett.

"I own a security company."

Deni looked down at the T-shirt she was wearing. "Yeah. I figured that much out, but it doesn't really tell me anything."

Gunner chuckled at the understatement of Price's response. "Sort of giving her the Spark's Notes version, aren't you? Price is CEO of one of the most prestigious and prosperous security firms out there. His list of clients would probably read like a who's who of the world's most rich and famous."

"Someone did their homework." Price didn't sound offended by Gunner's knowledge.

He shrugged. "I had some time to kill at Deni's apartment."

"And you ran a background check." Price actually looked impressed. "I did the same thing while Denise was showering. You graduated from Boston University with honors and a criminal justice degree. You were top of your class at the FBI Academy and you played rugby in high school."

Gunner grinned. He liked a pissing contest as much as the next guy. "Very good. You're left-handed, your mother is a distant cousin of Charlie Chaplin and you were born on March 11."

Price shook his head. "I may have to try to steal you away from the FBI. I could use a man with an eye for details."

"You're a Pisces," Deni muttered, looking at Price.

Price looked at her. "Excuse me?"

"Your birth sign. You're a Pisces, a water sign. I'm Leo, fire. Could be a tricky combination."

Gunner laughed. "Never pegged you as an astrology believer, Deni."

She shrugged. "I'm not actually. I was just feeling left out of the conversation."

Gunner gestured for her to continue. "Tell us more. And I should warn you now. I'm an earth sign."

Deni grinned. "A girl in one of my college classes was talking to her girlfriend about astrology once. Trying to explain that she'd dumped this guy because their signs weren't compatible. I was curious because this girl really seemed to put a lot of weight on the idea, so I checked a book out of the library and read up on it. Thought it was pretty fascinating."

Price leaned forward, looking intrigued. "So the signs are against us?"

She gave him a mischievous grin. "Possibly. Do you think the Grand Master takes astrological signs into account when he forms the threesomes?"

"Absolutely not."

Again, Gunner was struck by Price's certainty, but he let it go, continuing with the checklist of issues that still needed to be resolved. "So now that we've tackled the living situation, personal information and problematic horoscopes, maybe we should go ahead and acknowledge the elephant in the corner."

It occurred to Gunner that Deni wouldn't completely relax until the sex issue had been resolved. It had been hovering in the background all day. Perhaps they would all feel better if they knew the physical aspects of this odd relationship would work.

Deni frowned. "I don't understand."

Price rose and perched on the edge of the coffee table in front of her. "He's talking about sex, Denise."

"Oh." Deni ran her palms along her thighs, trying to tug the T-shirt down again.

Gunner grasped her hand. "You knew this was coming."

Price leaned forward. Gunner couldn't miss how tight their circle had grown. With any other man, Gunner would feel as if his personal space was being invaded. With Price and Deni, it felt comfortable. Normal.

Price claimed her free hand. "Why don't we move this conversation to the bedroom? We'd be more comfortable there."

Deni tried to tug her hands free, but neither man released her.

"Bedroom?"

Gunner pulled her to her feet. And then, because he hated seeing her so frightened, he wrapped her in his embrace. Deni's body was tense, rigid, but after a few moments, she released a long sigh, going soft in his arms. He placed a gentle kiss on the top of her head when she returned the hug and touched her hands lightly to the small of his back.

Price didn't move. Instead, he watched in silence. Gunner's

gaze connected with Price's and he saw approval in the other man's eyes. They were going to have to join forces and work together to alleviate Deni's anxiety.

God. A virgin. Deni had revealed that little secret to him a few months earlier. She'd actually been asking him for advice on how he thought she should go about losing it. It had taken all the strength in his body not to say to hell with the Trinity Masters and take her back to his place then and there, unwilling to think about another man touching her. Instead he'd told her she should wait for the right guy, hang in there until she found that special someone.

Now she was here and...shit. A virgin. What the hell was he supposed to do with that? He'd never had sex with an inexperienced woman. Maybe it would be easier if he didn't care so much about Deni, but the fact was he did care. A lot. It would kill him to hurt her, to cause her any pain, physically or emotionally.

He released her slowly and stepped back as Price moved forward. Price offered the same friendly, easy hug, but he took it to the next level, bending to kiss her.

Gunner had never considered himself a voyeur, but watching Price and Deni kiss, observing their tongues tangle as their hands stroked each other's faces and bodies sent his cock from emerging to erect in an instant. He adjusted the material of his pants, trying to find some relief from the sudden constriction.

When Price and Deni parted, he was there, dying for a taste. Deni moved back to him easily. He kissed her the way he'd wanted to for years. He was a starving man at the feast and nothing would hold him back now.

He tightened his grip in her hair with one hand as he drifted the other lower to cup her breast. Deni gasped, but he didn't offer her surcease, an out. He kept her lips pressed against his as he explored her body.

Deni jerked. Gunner opened his eyes, unsurprised to discover Price standing behind her, slowly lifting her T-shirt. Gunner moved back incrementally, allowing Price the room he needed to completely pull the soft cotton off. Deni hadn't bothered to put her bra back on after her shower. Without the shirt, she stood between them in nothing but her far-too-practical, plain white cotton panties. Gunner had never seen anything sexier.

Her skin flushed, a faint pink hue covering her cheeks and her chest. Gunner wasn't certain if it was embarrassment or arousal causing the blush. Probably a bit of both.

Deni tried to move closer to him, no doubt to hide. She had self-confidence when it came to her work—the woman knew her stuff—but it wasn't translating to her personal life.

He gently pushed her away, letting his gaze sweep over her body. Deni started to lift her hands, to use them as a shield, but Price grasped her wrists and pulled them behind her back. "Let us look at you, Denise."

She struggled for only a second, then, when it became apparent she was no match for Price's strength, she stilled.

Gunner ran his hands along her arms, her waist, her hips. Deni shivered at his touch. "You're so beautiful."

A crinkle appeared between her eyes as if she was trying to read the genuineness of his compliment. Given her unusual childhood, she'd missed too many experiences she should have had—prom and Homecoming dances, weekend dates and frat parties. Deni had spent her entire life between the pages of a book or trapped in a lab, running her damn trials. The world had passed her by as she lived alone inside her clever mind. It was time to draw her out. Show her what living was really about.

"Turn around." Price's deep-voiced command proved he was a man who was used to getting what he wanted. Gunner wondered how Deni would respond to Price's alpha ways. Hell, what would she think of his?

Her blush deepened, but she didn't move.

"Denise." Price released her hands and waited.

Gunner moved closer, whispering, "Be brave, Deni. You have nothing to hide from us."

She licked her lips nervously, and then twisted to face Price. Gunner noticed she kept her hands down, away from her body this time. As always, she was a quick study.

Price took his time, eating her alive with his eyes. When he finally spoke, his voice was gruff with emotion. "I want you."

Without waiting for a reply, Price leaned forward, picked her up and carried her to the bedroom. Gunner followed, pleased to see the large king-sized bed that awaited them. Neither he nor Price were small men. They would need plenty of room. Price placed Deni on her feet and stripped her panties away in one quick motion. Then he lifted her again and gently laid her in the center of the mattress.

Gunner reached up, loosened his tie and dragged it out of the collar as she watched.

Price began to disrobe as well. Deni's gaze traveled between them, quietly observing as they bared themselves to her.

As Gunner shed his boxers, he heard Deni's nervous intake of breath. Looking at her, it occurred to him she may never have seen a naked man before. Whenever Deni talked about growing up, she only mentioned her mother, never a father. One day soon, he'd ask her more about her family, her upbringing.

Now wasn't the time. His cock was hard enough to pound nails into concrete. A quick glance to the right proved Price was in a similar state.

When Price took a step toward the bed, Deni pushed herself up and pressed her back against the headboard. Her quick retreat stopped Price in his tracks.

They were doing this all wrong. When Deni was in their arms, when they kissed and touched her, she relaxed. They'd given her too much time to think. Gunner walked to the bed and sat next to her. He leaned against the wall as well, the two of them sitting side by side like two strangers waiting for a bus.

He reached out and clasped her hand in his. Price watched without joining them.

"Deni, you have nothing to be afraid of."

She frowned. "I'm not scared."

He grinned. She was a shitty liar.

Price sank down on the mattress near her feet. "Well, I am."

Deni's eyes widened. "You are?"

"I've never had sex with a virgin," Price confessed.

"So if I'd had sex before, you'd be doing things differently?"

Gunner nodded. "Yeah. A lot different."

Deni didn't reply immediately. "I don't want you to do that. I've been the odd guy out my whole life. I'm tired of it."

Gunner raised her hand and kissed it. "This isn't just about you. I've never participated in ménage sex either."

Price moved closer, crawling up the bed until he'd claimed Deni's other side. "Oh, I've done threesomes."

Deni laughed, the sound catching Gunner off-guard until she said, "Why am I not surprised?"

She squeezed his hand and then reached over to touch Price's face. "Tell you what. Let's forget the virginity thing and the ménage thing. Maybe we could just go with the flow. Figure out what feels right for us."

Price grinned. "I can handle that. What do you want to do first?"

"Can I touch you?" Her eyes drifted lower, giving away exactly what she was curious to explore.

Gunner moved until both he and Price were sitting in front of her. He lifted her hand and pressed her fingers against his chest. "I'm yours, Deni. You can do whatever you want."

She rubbed her hand along his pecs and shoulders, then repeated the same motions on Price's chest. She drifted her fingers lower but stopped short as her shyness reappeared. Price took away her choice. He grabbed her hand and wrapped her fingers around his cock.

Deni slowly stroked the hard flesh. Gunner wondered how Price was able to remain patient with her light touches. He shook his head. "No, Deni. Like this." He placed his hand on top of hers, the two of them wrapped around Price's erection.

Price narrowed his eyes and then groaned when Gunner showed her exactly how firmly she could rub him.

"Fuck," Price muttered. "That feels…" His voice faded away when Gunner encouraged Deni to grip Price's balls with her free hand. Then he added extra pressure.

"I'm not hurting him?"

Gunner shook his head. "You ever heard the song with the lyrics about something hurting so good? People are capable of finding pleasure through pain."

Price's gaze captured Deni's. "I'm going to show you exactly how that works."

"When?" Deni's tone betrayed her undeniable interest.

Gunner chuckled and then leaned forward and kissed her as they continued to rub their hands along Price's cock.

Price's breathing warned Gunner he was getting too close. Gunner loosened his grip on Deni's hand and then pulled her away from their lover.

Price put his sudden freedom to good use, tugging Deni's waist until she was lying on the mattress. Gunner continued kissing her as he gripped her hair, tightening his fingers in her soft tresses, building the pressure until Deni gasped. "Oh, I see."

Price leaned over her chest and took her nipple into his mouth, sucking on the distended flesh. Deni moaned.

Deni's caresses were timid at first. She rested her hands on Gunner's shoulders, but as the power of the moment grew, she became bolder, braver, wilder. She ran her fingers through his hair, reaching down with the other hand to stroke Price's face.

Gunner tried to understand the part of him that loved having Price in bed with them. He'd never looked at another man with anything even remotely close to desire. And while he didn't feel attracted to Price, he didn't mind their close contact or even Price's accidental brushes against him.

They were partners, working together to bring their spouse pleasure…and maybe help each other out along the way.

Gunner lowered his head and claimed Deni's other nipple. Price nipped at her breast while Gunner increased the suction. Deni lifted her hips and tightened her fingers in his hair until his scalp stung.

Price took them to the next level when he reached lower, rubbing her clit. Deni thrust against his fingers, begging for more.

"So wet." He heard Price murmur. He suspected his partner in lust was urging him on, as anxious as he was to bury himself inside their pretty little bride.

Gunner released her breast to kneel by her hip. He watched Price's fingers drive Deni's arousal higher, stroking her clit harder, faster.

"God, please," she cried.

Did she know what she was asking for?

Gunner reached out, desperate to feel her wet heat. He circled the entrance to her sex. Deni stilled, her chest rising and falling with her rapid breaths. She was close to coming, he could see it in her flushed face, her heavily lidded eyes. It wouldn't take much.

Gunner glanced at Price, who nodded.

"Do it," Price urged.

Gunner thrust two fingers inside Deni's tight pussy while Price continued caressing her clit. Deni stiffened, balling her hands into fists at her sides.

"Oh my God. Holy shit." Her words escaped in loud pants when he withdrew and then pressed back in. Her pussy clenched against his fingers, her eyes closing tightly.

"Gunner. Price." She screamed their names as they pushed her over, her orgasm striking hard and fast. Price acknowledged her pretty cries as he moved next to her and swallowed her soft mewls with gentle kisses.

Gunner's heart raced as he watched his partners.

Oh yeah. He could definitely do a lifetime of this.

CHAPTER FOUR

Deni clung to Price's shoulders, struggling to understand what had just happened. One minute she was sitting on the loveseat in the living room, so anxious she couldn't think straight. The next she was lying naked in bed with two of the most gorgeous men she'd ever met, having the greatest orgasm of her life.

And they hadn't even fucked her yet.

Her mind whirled.

Somewhere along the line, Gunner had moved to claim her other side, and she was currently the middle of a man sandwich. She giggled.

"Something funny?" Price asked.

She shook her head, unwilling to tell them her silly thoughts. "I'm just happy. But we're not done, are we? I mean neither of you..." She wasn't sure how to finish her comment. She could feel two very distinct erections pressing against her hips.

"We thought we'd give you a second to catch your breath." Gunner stroked her breast. Deni struggled not to make a sound.

Her skin was super sensitive and everything they did to her felt unbelievable. Amazing.

"Are you on birth control?"

Deni felt her face flush again. Leave it to Price to cut to the chase.

"I am."

She sensed Gunner's surprise.

"Why?"

She lifted one shoulder, not quite comfortable sharing so many personal details of her life. "My menstrual cycles were irregular and I used to experience bad cramps. The doctor suggested them and they work." She was careful to avoid eye contact with either man. She couldn't believe she was lying in bed naked with them, talking about her period.

"Do you remember to take it?"

Deni narrowed her eyes at Price's question. "Yes, I remember." Most of the time. She didn't say the last out loud. She never missed more than a day or two, and she always corrected the oversight the way the doctor told her to.

"Did you take today's?"

Price was like a dog with a bone. He seemed convinced she'd lose her own head if it wasn't attached.

She nodded and then paused. Had she? "I think so." Then she remembered taking it in her office as part of her breakfast regimen of a too-ripe banana and a cup of coffee. God, had it really only been this morning that she'd been in her lab, working away as if her entire life wasn't about to take a wide right turn? "Yes. I did. I absolutely did."

Price kissed her. "Good. I'm not using a condom."

Gunner lifted his head. "Price..."

"I'm clean. You?"

Gunner nodded.

"Then this conversation is over. She's ours. We're hers. I'm not putting anything between us. If you want to, that's your call to make."

"Does everything about today feel completely weird to anyone else, or is it just me?" While Deni had spent nearly every second since Price walked into her lab struggling to adjust, neither man displayed the slightest bit of unease or confusion or...hell...anything.

Gunner pressed a quick kiss on her shoulder. "It's all odd, Deni. But that doesn't mean it's wrong."

"I'm not saying that. It's just—"

Price interrupted her. "I understand what you mean. You and I are jumping into this relationship in the middle. Most couples have a definite beginning where they play the dating game. They get to know each other slowly, in safe places like restaurants and movie theaters. You and Gunner got to do a bit of that. Meanwhile, we skipped the preliminaries, hopped into bed within hours of meeting, talking about birth control and masturbating while—"

"Masturbating?" Gunner asked.

Price chuckled. "You missed that part."

Gunner looked like he wanted specifics, but Price continued. "Regardless of how strange this situation is, I'm not sure I've ever been in a relationship that felt more natural. More honest."

Deni wanted to agree, but she had no comparison. A quick glance at Gunner's face confirmed he felt the same way as Price. She'd take their word for it, because the simple truth was she trusted them.

Apparently the time for talking had passed. Gunner sat up, moving her legs apart and kneeling between them. As she looked into his beloved face, she recognized the power of this moment. And how much she wanted these men.

She'd told herself she would never experience love. She was

wrong. She would fall in love with them. She probably was already there with Gunner, and there was something about Price that called to her, touched her.

Price rose and stood beside the bed. His gaze never left her face as Gunner leaned forward, placing his cock at the entrance of her sex. She sucked in a deep breath as Gunner slowly pressed in.

There was a twinge of discomfort, then a stinging pain. Deni tried to mask her slight wince, but she clearly failed. Price frowned as Gunner froze.

"Don't stop," she whispered.

Gunner studied her face and then he continued to move until he was seated to the hilt.

"Okay?" he asked.

She nodded and then grinned. "Guess I'm not a virgin anymore."

Gunner didn't immediately agree. She gasped when he started to pull out, the sudden movement catching her by surprise.

He didn't stop until he'd completely withdrawn. She was confused until she watched him stepped aside so Price could take his place.

"Oh," she said softly as Price entered her. Like Gunner, he left her feeling uncomfortably full. She'd have to research the male anatomy, determine if her men were a bit larger than the norm.

Price leaned forward and kissed her. "Ours," he murmured against her lips.

She smiled, no longer feeling threatened by his undeniable claiming. "Mine," she declared.

Price moved back the slightest bit and then pushed in faster.

Deni released a completely unladylike squeak and

wrapped her legs around Price's waist, urging him to do it again.

Price complied, thrusting in and out for at least a dozen strokes. The twinges of discomfort gave way to pure pleasure.

Then Price left her and Gunner took his place, driving her farther, higher. Her fingernails dug into Gunner's back and he hissed with pain. She recalled his comment about good hurts. This one must have qualified because he increased his speed, groaning in obvious desire.

She cried out when Gunner left her again, but Price didn't give her time to miss him, picking up the same maddening, beautiful rhythm.

Deni looked over and watched as Gunner stroked his own cock, his eyes glued to the place where Price entered her.

Price had said they would share her. She hadn't fully understood what that meant until this moment. When Gunner reached over to touch her clit, Deni knew she wouldn't last much longer.

Price increased his speed, pumping harder as Gunner stroked her. Deni closed her eyes, struggling not to fly away. It was too much. Too good.

Mercifully, Price gave her permission to let go. "I'm not going to last much longer, Denise. Come with me."

It was all she needed to hear. Her back arched as lightning struck. Price stiffened above her, a stream of curse words flowing from his lips. "Jesus Christ. So fucking good. Shit. Shit, Denise."

Mere seconds passed before Price pulled out and collapsed next to her and Gunner returned to take his place. The head of his cock nudged her and then he stopped.

Deni opened her eyes as Gunner leaned over her.

"Sore?"

She was touched by his concern. And while she was definitely feeling twinges of pain in unique places, she would never tell Gunner. She didn't want this moment to end.

She shook her head. "No."

"Liar," he whispered.

She grinned, cupping his handsome face. "Don't you dare stop."

He slid in slowly, his path eased by her arousal and Price's come. He moved slowly, giving her time to recover, to regroup.

Gunner moved slowly, his face reflective of someone savoring the moment. Deni smiled, tears forming in her eyes. She didn't realize how powerful this experience would be. How perfect.

Price leaned closer, tugging on her jaw so she faced him. "Crying?"

Gunner stopped moving, but she shook her head, tried to pull him closer with her legs around his waist. "Happy."

Gunner chuckled and began thrusting deeper, faster.

Deni tried to catch her breath as the telltale tingles started in her pussy. Again? She didn't think it was possible. Physical exhaustion was claiming her and yet her body wanted more. Would it always be this way with them?

Price gave her a long, slow, extremely thorough kiss as his hand gently caressed her breast. Gunner's motions became harder, less graceful. He was getting close. So was she.

Price rubbed her clit—the clever bastard had found her self-destruct button—and she broke away from his kiss, struggling to suck in air as her body gave way to another orgasm.

Gunner came with her. Dropping to his elbows, he caged her beneath him, his lips and tongue traveling over her sensitive skin in a way that felt almost reverent.

He withdrew slowly and she couldn't restrain the shivers his departure produced. Every part of her body was on system overload.

Gunner twisted her as he claimed the other side of the bed, shifting her so that he could spoon her from behind. Price lay facing her. He dragged one of her legs over his and nuzzled closer. None of them bothered to pull up the sheet or blanket. There was enough heat between the three of them that such things weren't necessary.

Gunner placed a sleepy kiss on her shoulder and then she listened as his breathing turned deep, heavy. Price cupped her face, simply staring at her.

"I wasn't happy when I got that letter," he confessed.

She smiled. "I know. I don't blame you. I had pencils in my hair."

"I was wrong."

It was three very simple words. Taken apart they would mean little. Spoken now, together, by Price... Deni wasn't sure she'd ever heard anything more beautiful.

A lump formed in her throat, making it impossible for her to reply. What the hell could she say? He and Gunner had taken her from her safe, boring world and shown her Heaven. Thank you seemed insignificant, almost trivial.

As always, she waited too long, forgot to speak out loud.

Price grinned. "Go to sleep, Denise."

"Good night," she whispered, closing her eyes. Usually her mind raced a mile a minute each night as she lay down. She'd spend at least an hour playing over her experiments, analyzing data, plotting out her next day's course. She jokingly told Curtis she did her best thinking in bed and the shower. He'd told her that was a sad state of affairs. She didn't understand why he felt that way at the time. Now she did.

She rested her head on Price's shoulder when he shifted to his back and snuggled closer.

Then she fell asleep.

. . .

Deni opened her eyes, surprised by the bright sunlight filling the room. Typically she woke before dawn, anxious and ready to start the workday. She'd slept hours later than normal.

Heavy breathing coming from both sides reminded her why. Glancing to her left, she saw Price sacked out on his back, one arm thrown above his head, the other lying across his chest. Her dark, dangerous-looking warrior appeared almost peaceful. The sheet drifted low, only covering him from the waist down. She was tempted to lift it, to peek beneath to see if he was hard. She resisted, too afraid she'd wake him.

Looking right, Gunner lay on his stomach, his face turned toward her. His jaw was covered with a shadow of a beard, and she realized she'd never seen him looking anything less than completely put together. She preferred this version of the man with his mussed-up hair and scruffy beard. He was real. Handsome.

Hers.

Deni needed to get a grip. Needed time to figure out what the hell she was supposed to do now. It would be too easy for her to disappear into these men, into this unusual, but highly addictive relationship. She squeezed her legs together, relishing the slight ache in her muscles.

She should have taken a bath last night. Indulged in a nice long soak to clear away the confusion and clean up the stickiness. They'd all fallen asleep immediately following their orgasms.

She sat up slowly and made her way to the bottom of the bed carefully so she didn't wake them up. She'd get a shower, get dressed—in the same damn jeans and T-shirt—then head over to the lab. A few hours away from the hotel and Gunner and Price would give her time to put her thoughts together.

Deni tiptoed to her room and locked the door behind her. She didn't trust her men not to follow her, to take her plans and toss them out on their ear. After her shower, she pulled her hair into a ponytail, got dressed and threw her shoes on. She listened through the door but didn't hear anyone.

With any luck, Gunner and Price would sleep a while longer. She knew what she was doing was dangerous, but she needed to get back to the lab. Her heart raced as she grabbed the keycard and headed for the door to the hallway. If she could just make it to the lab safely, she'd talk to the director about beefing up security. God, she would never do anything so stupid if she weren't at such a vital place in her research, but it couldn't be helped. She needed to go.

She opened the door and then gasped, jumping back. Price leaned on the doorframe.

"Going somewhere?" he asked.

She narrowed her eyes. "Work."

He shook his head. "Bad girl."

"Dammit, Price, I told you last night I needed—"

"I told you," Price interrupted, "that you're not going anywhere for the next couple days. And after that, you're not walking around without either Gunner or me with you. Someone is trying to kill you, Denise."

She rolled her eyes and tried to play off what she knew was a real and present threat. "Don't be dramatic. Everything so far has just been scare tactics, nothing more."

Price scowled and walked into her room, pushing her farther in with each step.

Yeah. That didn't work.

Price closed the door behind him but didn't stop until he'd backed her against the bed. Deni, unable to retreat any more, sat. Price towered over her.

"I hardly call a bomb a scare tactic. It was a serious threat, and if you refuse to treat it as such, then perhaps Gunner and I need to change our approach toward protecting you."

She didn't like the sound of that. "What do you mean?"

"If you refuse to cooperate, we're going to have to treat you as subordinate. A captive."

"You wouldn't dare."

"Actually we would." Gunner's voice startled her, coming from the door that connected to the rest of the suite. Somehow he'd unlocked it.

"Take off your clothes, Denise."

Her gaze flew back to Price. "What?"

"Get undressed. Now."

There was a hard, demanding edge to his voice that left no doubt in Deni's mind she would be finishing this conversation naked. "Why?"

Gunner walked into the room. "Deni. Do it now."

She struggled to understand the compulsion that had her reaching for the hem of her T-shirt. She'd never had problems with people in positions of authority. Hell, she'd been at the mercy of others for most of her career—the lab director, the executive committee who controlled much of what her facility did, colleagues with seniority, research lobbyist, politicians. She played the game in order to protect her research.

But this was different. Wasn't it?

"We're losing her again."

Gunner's comment captured her attention and she realized she'd frozen in the middle of pulling off her shirt, baring herself only to her midriff.

"Does she do that a lot?" Price asked.

Gunner grinned and nodded. "Our Deni's a thinker. One of these days, I'm hoping she'll start sharing some of those deep thoughts out loud instead of disappearing into her head."

Deni pulled her shirt back down. Price scowled and made a deep sound of disapproval. "Wrong way."

"Why do you want me to take my clothes off?" Deni didn't

have problems following orders if the reasons why they were issued were explained to her.

"Gunner's going to take your outfit and hide it."

Price's answer confused her even more. "Why would he do that?"

"You can't leave the hotel room if you're naked. Given your attempt to escape this morning, this seems the easiest way to ensure your compliance. Plus, it provides some eye candy for Gunner and me."

Deni was mortified. "You don't seriously expect me to walk around this hotel room completely nude all day, do you?"

Price reached for her T-shirt and stripped it over her head with ease. "Yes. I do."

Gunner had moved forward during their conversation and was kneeling behind where she sat on the bed. He made quick work of her bra and added it to the pile.

Topless, Deni covered her breasts with one hand while trying to fend off her lovers with the other.

Gunner grasped her and wrapped his arms around her, preventing her from using her hands. When Price reached for the button on her jeans, she kicked out, her last-ditch attempt.

Price sidestepped her kick easily, then pinned her legs to the side of the bed with his. Once he'd unfastened her pants, Gunner lifted her slightly to allow Price to tug them and her panties off. The entire disrobing had taken less than a minute.

She was completely outnumbered. "I think it's only fair that you two take off your clothes too."

Gunner chuckled. "No. We're not trying to escape."

She twisted, trying to break his hold. "What if I get cold?"

"We'll crank up the heat." Gunner released her, but her freedom was short-lived. Price leaned forward. Deni resisted the urge to back away from his angry face.

Last night, he'd been kind, even sweet in his own way.

Today she was facing the man she'd met in her lab. He was irritated, scowling, looking far too serious.

Before she could move, a knock sounded on the door in the living suite.

"That will be breakfast. Price and I ordered room service. I'll get it." Gunner stood, gathered her clothing and started to leave her room. He stopped at the doorway. "Unless you'd prefer to sign for it, Deni."

She smirked at his joke and he laughed, mercifully shutting the door behind him. Standing naked in front of Gunner and Price was one thing. She didn't intend to offer a peep show to every hotel employee as well.

She released a slow breath and then glanced up. Price hadn't moved. Maybe she should have signed for the food. That task would have been simpler than facing Price.

While Gunner had taken her attempt to leave in stride, Price was genuinely furious.

"I'm sorry." She wasn't sure what else to say. She hated it when people were mad at her.

Price sat on the bed next to her. "Do you understand the purpose of the Trinity Masters?"

Deni nodded. "Of course I do. The vision is that there's power in three. By forming triads, the Grand Master hopes to build strong relationships that will lead to the success of our country and humankind. The Trinity Masters have been instrumental in influencing the continued development of technology, education, the military and medicine."

"That's right." Price took her hand. "You're special, Denise."

She frowned. She'd heard that line too often in her lifetime. Sometimes it was a compliment. Most of the time it wasn't. She rolled her eyes. "Great."

He tightened his grip, squeezing her fingers in a way she

assumed was meant to soothe her. "I don't mean that as an insult."

"I'm sure you don't, but I'm pretty sick of hearing it just the same." She mimicked her younger self. "Why can't I go to third grade with my friends?" Then she adopted her mother's voice. "Because you're special, Deni. Why can't I go to summer camp instead of taking a college class? Because you're special."

Deni threw her hands up, flopping back on the mattress. "I'm fucking sick of being special. I just want to be normal."

Price lay down next to her and rested his hand on her bare stomach. Just like that, Deni went from pissed off to turned on. She never would have pegged herself as a sexual creature, but Price and Gunner had certainly ignited something inside her, and she didn't see it burning out any time soon.

"There's no one in the entire world who's normal, Denise. We're all just our own brand of unique."

"So why do you think I'm special?"

"It's never apparent why the Grand Master partners people up immediately, but he does have a plan."

Deni hadn't had time to consider why the Grand Master had thrust Gunner and Price into her life. All she knew was she was glad he had. "What do you think his plan is for us?"

Price lifted one shoulder. "I'm not sure where Gunner fits in, but I think my role is to protect you."

Deni didn't think that sounded like much of a power match. "That seems flimsy."

He turned to face her, his upper body propped up by his elbow. "Not really. I genuinely believe you're going to make a difference in the world with your research. Tell me about the studies you do. What's your long-term goal?"

"To find a cure for neurological disorders. Alzheimer's, Parkinson's, ALS. We're still a long way away from that, but I really believe that we'll get there."

He nodded. "And the way there is through stem-cell research?"

"Yes, as well as through epigenetics."

Price lifted his shoulder. "I've never heard of that."

"Epigenetics is a fairly new and potentially invaluable field of research that looks at genes as being switches. Meaning they can be turned on and off by both environmental and chemical signals. Epigenetic gene control is a likely culprit for the causes of both Alzheimer's and Parkinson's. The human genome was sequenced in 2003, but the human epigenome is an even larger feat. Even so, it holds huge promise."

"And people are against that?"

Deni sighed. "There are some people who are against the use of human embryos in stem-cell research. Period. Then there are some pro-lifers who think we should only use adult stem cells. It all lies with when a person sees life beginning. At fertilization? Gastrulation? With the first organ derived from morphogenesis? The first twitch of a newly active cardiac cell?"

Price shook his head. "When did we stop speaking English?"

Deni laughed. "Basically what people fail to realize is that adult stem cells are only pluripotent. That means they can only differentiate into some but not all types of tissues. Researchers need totipotent cells, ones that can become any other cell in the body through chemical signaling. IPSC have their benefit, but they're expensive and hard to come by."

"IPSC?"

"Induced pluripotent stem cells."

"Where do the human embryos come from?"

"Lots of places, but mainly from in vitro clinics. They're embryos that have been stored too long or that are slated to be destroyed anyway."

Price ran his hand through her hair. "That sounds harmless enough."

Deni hadn't been touched much in her life and never like this. It made her feel hot and fuzzy and dizzy all at the same time. She cleared her throat and forced herself to pay attention to the conversation at hand.

"Let's face it, Price. There are a million different aspects of my research that have been debated endlessly. Lots of people are of the opinion that once a cell or tissue leaves your body, it isn't yours anymore. Look at Henrietta Lacks. She unknowingly gave up her cells in 1951 and they've been dividing her ever since. Her cells have played a role in the cure for polio as well as establishing legal laws regarding the ethical treatment of prisoners. Hell, they've even been to the moon and back to study the effects of anti-gravity on cell division."

Price sighed. "So basically this is just yet another area where religion and science clash."

Deni nodded. "In a nutshell, I guess."

"And these threats against you are likely to remain as long as you continue your research?"

Deni closed her eyes wearily. "I don't think what's happening to me is normal. There are a lot of scientists in the same field who don't come home to destroyed apartments and bombs."

Price cupped her jaw, turned her toward him. She opened her eyes, touched by the concern written on his face.

"You've ticked off a dangerous person. My job is to protect. I sometimes wondered if I hadn't been partnered up in a triad because I didn't bring enough to the table."

"Don't be silly."

He grinned. "You're mine, Denise. You're brilliant, talented and passionate. I'm going to keep you safe so that you can finish your work. Save the world."

She laughed. "Wow. No pressure there."

He kissed her.

"Must be nice to know your place in this relationship."

Price and Deni sat up at the sound of Gunner's voice. It was apparent he'd been standing in the doorway, listening. "Meanwhile, I don't have a clue why I'm here."

"Comic relief?" Price suggested.

Deni giggled and stood. "If I promise not to leave, can I at least get a T-shirt?"

Gunner and Price said, "No," in unison.

"Come on. Breakfast is getting cold." Gunner took Deni's hand and led her to the table where they'd eaten dinner last night. They each claimed the same seats, falling into comfortable patterns.

Would it always be this simple?

Deni suspected not. There were still too many bridges to cross. "What do we tell people about us?"

Price paused in the middle of buttering a croissant. "It's imperative that we keep the true nature of our relationship a secret."

Deni took a sip of orange juice. "I know. So how do we explain the three of us living together in your house?"

Gunner leaned back. "I'm still not sure I can get the transfer to Boston. It may just be the two of you for a while."

"You'll get the transfer."

"How do you know so much about the inner workings of the Trinity Masters, Price? This is the third time you've alluded to knowing something more than Deni and I."

"The Trinity Masters isn't run by one man."

Deni put down her fork. "It isn't? I thought the Grand Master held all the power."

Price shook his head. "Ultimately, all decisions are made by the Grand Master, but there is a triumvirate standing behind him. Three members who support him, offer counsel, handle day-to-day issues that may arise."

"You're one of those three?" Gunner asked.

Price nodded.

"But you didn't know about us, about the ceremony," Deni said.

"I suspect the Grand Master knew I would be resistant to this particular match. I would have fought him on it because I didn't understand the reasons behind it."

It was the first time Deni felt as if she shared a common trait with her self-assured, powerhouse lover. Neither of them could easily accept commands without also being offered reasons.

"So you know who the Grand Master is." Gunner's curiosity was almost palpable. Deni didn't share it. It had never bothered her not to know the man's identity.

Price grinned. "Is it the CIA or the FBI who coined the line, I could tell you, but then I'd have to kill you?"

Gunner snorted. "I think it actually came from some damn spy movie."

"My mother will never believe that you and I are a couple, Price." Deni tried to steer their conversation back to important matters.

Price covered his heart with his hand, pretending to be wounded. "What? She never pictured her little girl with a billionaire playboy?"

Deni laughed. "Afraid not." She glanced at Gunner. "But she would believe I was dating you. You're the only person who's ever really stuck around, been a friend."

Gunner shook his head. "I'm always surprised when you say that. You're gorgeous and funny enough that it's not completely impossible to overlook your nerd tendencies."

Deni tore a crust off her bread and lobbed it at Gunner's head. "Jerk," she teased.

"So you and Gunner will be the couple, and eventually you should get married to solidify the union."

"What about you?" Gunner asked.

"I have more money than God. I think that entitles me to be a bit eccentric. I'll take a sudden interest in stem-cell research, become very good friends with one of the field's top scientists and her boyfriend. I'll build Denise a lab on my property with a connecting house for the two of you. My staff is well trained and trustworthy. We'll make this work."

Deni was amazed by Price's quick response. She'd never met anyone so self-assured, so confident.

"Sounds like a plan," Gunner said.

She studied his face, wondering if he was truly okay with Price's proposal. Gunner seemed to take everything in stride, accepting their new fate so easily. She wished she could roll with the punches as well as he did. Instead, she felt like she was struggling to keep up.

"Can I borrow your phone?" she asked Gunner.

Gunner handed his cell over without question. Deni dialed the number to her lab, certain Curtis would be there and wondering where the hell she was. Sure enough, he answered on the second ring.

She took a few minutes assuring Curtis she wasn't dying. Poor man couldn't think of any other reason for her absence. Once she calmed him down regarding her health, she gave him detailed instructions on what she needed him to do over the course of the next two days. With any luck, she'd convince her so-called captors to release her by then.

"Thanks, Curtis. See you in a few days." She clicked the phone off and returned it to Gunner.

"Feel better?" Gunner asked.

She nodded.

Gunner laid his phone on the table. "I'm surprised you didn't try to give him some coded message that would alert him you were being held against your will."

"How do you know I didn't? Maybe all that science-speak was nonsense and only Curtis is smart enough to figure it out. I bet he's on the phone with the police as we speak."

Gunner laughed. "Police? Yeah. I'm not worried."

"Finished eating?" Price asked, putting down his fork.

She nodded, and it occurred to her she'd eaten the entire meal in the nude while Gunner and Price were fully dressed. Where had her shyness gone? Why did this suddenly not feel so strange?

Price glanced at Gunner and then back at her. "Good. I think it's time we deal with your punishment."

She frowned. "I thought losing my clothes was the punishment."

Gunner grinned. "Nope. That was just a perk for us."

She started to stand, wondering if she could make it to her bedroom without being caught. Of course, considering the fact Gunner had managed to unlock her locked door, she wasn't sure what good running would do.

Price rose and pressed her back into her seat, his hands remaining firmly planted on her shoulders. "Don't move unless we tell you to."

Deni bit her lip, aware of the arousal Price's command had provoked. Her nipples tightened, her pussy grew damp.

Price dragged her chair away from the table, twisting it until she was facing the rest of the room, completely exposed.

Gunner moved to stand in front of her. "Put your feet around the legs of the chair."

She complied without asking why. Something told her the

only answers she was going to get in the next hour or four would be presented physically rather than verbally.

Gunner reached into his back pocket and Deni gasped when he produced a pair of handcuffs. He handed them to Price who pulled her wrists behind her back and snapped them into place.

Within seconds, they had her open and restrained. Deni's heart raced. Excitement tinged with the tiniest bit of fear coursed through her. She couldn't wait to see what they'd do next.

Gunner knelt in front of her and softly caressed her knees as he looked up at her. "Sore?"

She shook her head. He didn't seem to buy her answer, so she added, "Not really."

He nodded. "Scared?"

She grinned, shaking her head again. "Of you? No."

She thought he'd laugh, but instead his face grew more serious. "You should be."

His words caught her unaware until she recognized something in his face she'd never noticed before. Given her previous inexperience, she wondered if it had always been there, but she hadn't known what it was.

Gunner was looking at her with a hunger that took her breath away. "Oh."

"I can't always promise you easy, Deni. I want you too much."

She blinked rapidly and then realized Price's hands were still on her shoulders, his fingers tightening. Last night this had all seemed so much simpler. They were kind, careful with her.

Now, in the bright light of day, she could see all too well what she'd signed on for. Life with two powerful, dominant, physical men. Could she handle that?

She closed her eyes. The best way to find an answer was to experiment. "Show me," she whispered.

Her request unlocked the floodgates as four large, strong hands took over. Gunner pushed her legs farther apart, digging his fingers into the globes of her ass to drag her closer to the chair's edge. Then he bent his head and thrust his tongue inside her sex.

Deni groaned, her head falling back. The sensation of Gunner's mouth on her pussy, nipping at her clit, stroking her, would have been overwhelming enough, but he wasn't the only man in the room.

Price leaned over, kissing her upside down. It would have felt whimsical, almost fun, if Price's hands weren't upping the ante. He cupped her breasts, squeezing the flesh firmly before moving in for the kill. He took her nipples between his fingers, pinching lightly at first and then adding more pressure.

Deni tried to pull her face away from his, tried to gasp in some much needed air, but Price growled, releasing one of her breasts to grip her head, to hold her in place. He bit her lower lip and then soothed the soreness with his tongue.

Gunner added his fingers to the game, roughly pushing two inside her. She jerked and would have fallen off the chair if her men weren't holding her in place.

Pure physical hunger gave way to intelligent thought. Deni gave up trying to understand, to catalog, to piece this together. Some things couldn't be reasoned out. It was passionate, perfect.

Deni came as they continued to touch her. Then one orgasm gave way to a second. Price released the handcuffs and massaged her shoulders.

Gunner stood and took off his pants. "I want your mouth on me."

She licked her lips and moved forward, starving for a taste.

Gunner gripped her upper arms. "Wait. Not here."

He led her to the loveseat. Sinking onto the cushions, he tossed a pillow on the floor and directed Deni to kneel on it between his outstretched legs. No sooner had she bent her head closer, then Price joined her on the floor.

He tugged her hips back, nudging her sex with the head of his cock. She was wet, so he slid in easily. After the initial pain of their claiming last night, she'd come to realize she was made for these men, their bodies fit.

She grasped Gunner's cock, sucking the head into her mouth as Price pushed in to the hilt. Gunner cupped her head as he taught her what he liked. She tried to learn, but Price was doing his best to distract her.

His thrusting started slow and deep, but as the heat of the moment grew, so did his speed and strength. Deni followed suit, taking more and more of Gunner into her mouth.

Gunner tightened his fingers in her hair as Price gripped her hips, fighting for more leverage. It was all too much. Too good.

Deni stiffened a mere second before Gunner said, "Fuck, baby. I'm going to come."

She refused to release him, dying to taste. Gunner erupted and she swallowed as the last remnants of her climax shuddered through her.

Price stilled. "God damn. That's hot. Watching you suck his cock. Listening to both of you as you come. Fuck. A man could get addicted to this."

Deni continued to suckle on Gunner's cock though it grew soft. Gunner pulled her away, running his fingers along her cheek. "You're beautiful."

She smiled. She'd lived a lifetime without hearing those words. Deni didn't comprehend how much she'd longed for them until that moment.

Price leaned forward and placed a kiss on her back. It was then she realized he still hadn't come.

"Want me to stop?"

She shook her head, pressing her hips more firmly against him. "Never."

He chuckled and began to thrust once more. "Well, don't worry. This isn't going to take long."

Price was true to his word. Within a dozen strokes, he was there—jets of hot come filling her. Her eyes had closed as drowsiness came to claim her.

She wasn't sure which man carried her to the bedroom. All she knew was she was between their hard bodies once more.

The research was complete. This was where she was meant to be.

CHAPTER FIVE

Price splashed water into his face and ran his hands along his cheeks and jaw, enjoying the feeling of being clean-shaven. He'd spent three days holed up in the hotel with Gunner and Denise, none of them anxious to return to the real world after nearly sixty hours spent in a haze of sexual bliss.

Unfortunately, reality was a bitch and she held all the cards. He had to attend a meeting with the Bennett Securities stockholders today and he couldn't miss it.

Gunner had received a call from his supervisor at work earlier. He was needed back in D.C. the day after tomorrow.

Gunner had convinced Denise to allow him to accompany her to the lab today. He planned to set up his laptop and catch up on some work while watching over her. They'd convinced her to hand more duties over to her research assistant, Curtis, just in case she was forced to go into hiding again. Price was uneasy allowing her to return to work. Gunner's friend in the Boston FBI office, Jasper Young, had questioned Denise about the break-in at her apartment. The bomb recovered was what

Agent Young referred to as a run-of-the-mill YouTube variety that didn't have much more power than a firecracker.

Denise took that news to mean she was in the clear. She told Agent Young about her run-in with the Reverend. Young knew of the man, claimed he was an amateur terrorist with more followers than sense. He'd stressed that while the man's past offenses included arson, disturbing the peace and vandalism, it didn't mean he shouldn't be considered a serious threat.

Of course, Denise had failed to hear that part. She'd focused instead on the information that he wasn't a killer, using it to justify her belief there was no reason she couldn't return to the lab.

Price walked out of the bathroom, retrieved his suitcase from the bed and carried it to the living room of the suite.

Gunner and Denise were there, waiting. His driver would drop them off at the lab before taking him on to his office. They'd agreed to move from the hotel to his house today. Price was excited about the prospect of moving Denise and Gunner into his childhood home. He'd spent too many years alone in the huge mansion he'd inherited following his parents' deaths. It was past time for the rambling place to become a home again, complete with his partners and—God willing—children.

"Ready?" he asked.

Denise nodded as she lifted her hair, securing it into a ponytail. She'd bought a pair of dress slacks and a pretty blue blouse from the small boutique located in the hotel lobby.

Price had sent his personal assistant with two of his best security guards to sift through the remains of Denise's belongings and pack up whatever could be saved. He intended to surprise her tonight with what they'd found. His assistant assured him they'd recovered over half of Denise's wardrobe, quite a few undamaged books and a box full of pictures and other knick-knacks that hadn't been harmed. He hoped having some of her own things would make the move to his place easier for her.

Gunner picked up his laptop and suitcase. He'd stow his stuff in the trunk and the driver would deliver it to Price's house. "Sort of looking forward to seeing how the other half lives, Price. It's been a real hardship for me these past thirty-two years, brushing my own teeth and wiping my own ass. Looking forward to handing the task over to one of your umpteen thousand servants. Not going to lie. I've harbored more than a few French-maid fantasies."

Price grinned while Denise slapped Gunner on the arm. "Watch it, hotshot. The Grand Master said no straying."

Gunner winked at her and grabbed her ass. "Deni, with you in my bed, do you really think I'd have the energy to cheat? Not to sound crass, but my cock is sore from three straight days of fucking you. I'm going to have to go back to D.C. just to recover."

Price didn't admit it, but he felt the same way. They'd been insatiable.

Gunner tickled Denise, making her laugh. Only three days in and Price suspected Gunner was well on his way to becoming his best friend. Price didn't usually trust others easily. He could count on one hand the number of close friends he'd had in his lifetime. Typically, money got in the way. Price had been born with several silver spoons in his mouth. As a result, he'd met more than his fair share of fortune-seekers, men —and women—who'd offered friendship and then held out their hands for more.

Gunner didn't seem impressed by Price's wealth. Instead, he'd actually begun to tease Price about it, good-natured ribbing. Price realized Gunner was one of those rare people who had a knack for looking straight into someone's soul and seeing them for who they really were. No doubt it made him a crack FBI agent.

But it also made him a good person. Gunner had dug beneath Denise's eccentricities and offered her friendship at a time when she didn't have anyone. Now, he had done the same for Price. He'd burrowed beneath the tough-guy exterior and accepted Price's need for control, his overzealous desire to run the show. Gunner had been willing to follow his lead at first, averting what could have turned into a nasty pissing contest.

However, time was proving Gunner had just as many—if not more—alpha qualities as he did. Price suspected Gunner had swallowed some of his own pride initially to make things easier for Denise. For that, Gunner had earned Price's unwavering respect and admiration.

They may have come from different backgrounds, but they had one definite commonality—to love and protect Denise. That goal strengthened the bond between them.

"Come on." They grabbed their stuff and left the hotel room. Price squinted at the bright sunlight when they hit the street and it occurred to him he hadn't been outside since the day of the introduction ceremony. Some honeymoon, he thought with a grin.

Roman opened the door as they approached the limo. Price gave his driver instructions and then he joined his partners inside.

"One of these days we're going to have to initiate the limo," Gunner said, running his hands along the cool leather seat.

"Another fantasy?" Denise asked.

He nodded. "Hell, yeah. I've had a thousand fantasies about you these past few years, Deni. Looking forward to making them a reality."

"Really? Fantasies about me?"

Price shook his head. Denise still struggled to accept they

were both unquestionably attracted to her. He wondered how long it would take before she became self-confident with her looks, her sex appeal. She may have come to their relationship a virgin, but in three days she'd shed her inhibitions in the bedroom, unleashing a wild side that took them all by surprise.

"Yep. Lots of them. I've imagined us on the beach, in a limo, in the bathroom of some ritzy restaurant, too horny to wait until we get home. I've even pictured me bending you over that counter in your lab and burying myself inside you from behind."

Denise squeezed her legs together, obviously affected by Gunner's descriptions.

Unfortunately, they had the opposite effect on Price. "No sex without me." He wasn't sure where the words had come from, but he didn't like the idea of Denise and Gunner finding their pleasure if he wasn't there as well. They would be alone for hours in the lab today and, if the past three days were any indication, it would be damn near impossible for them to keep their hands off each other. The request was unreasonable, impractical. Undeniable.

Gunner narrowed his eyes, studying Price's face. There was no way Price could soften his features, take away the threat he was certain his new friend could see there. "You realize I'm returning to D.C. in two days. There's no telling how long it'll be before I can come back to Boston. Is this really a line in the sand you want to draw?"

Price considered what he would be giving up. Gunner would expect the same promise from him in return. He knew that. Even so, he couldn't let go of the feeling that it would be wrong for him to sleep with Denise without Gunner there. Maybe it would fade with time, but for now...

"I'm sure."

Gunner's frown disappeared, replaced by his usual

pleasant smile. "Good. I feel the same way."

"So do I," Deni whispered.

Gunner leaned his head against the back of the seat. "Damn. I'm afraid we're all in for some long nights."

"And cold showers," Price added.

"I don't know about that. Let's face it. You're both going to jack off, so I think I might expand on my masturbating skills. Maybe buy myself a vibrator." Denise's face reflected pure mischief. She obviously took joy in taunting them, proud of her ability to make such a dirty joke without blushing.

Price pulled her closer, cupping her face firmly in his hands. "No toys."

"What? No way. That's not fair."

"Fingers are one thing, Denise, but you're not using any toys to get yourself off."

She frowned and it took all the strength Price had not to laugh. God, they'd unleashed a sex maniac. And she was all theirs. She didn't reply. Price watched as her mind searched for some loophole. He was becoming accustomed to her long lapses into silence. Denise was a thinker who struggled to put things into words. He could only assume that came from being an only child and spending years alone without friends her own age.

"Denise. Promise me."

"I was sort of hoping to try a vibrator. I wanted to see what it felt like."

Price grinned. "Fair enough. We'll buy one and use it on you tonight."

Her face brightened. "Really?"

Gunner groaned. "You two are going to have to stop talking or we're going to have to instruct your driver to take a few dozen laps around the block while we take care of this."

Price glanced at the obvious erection in Gunner's pants.

Nice to know he wasn't alone in his arousal. They'd all come no more than two hours ago and already Price felt restless, hungry, horny.

He'd been wrong to demand that they limit their sexual interludes to times when they were all there.

"We're here." Denise reached for her messenger bag as the limo pulled up outside her work. "I'm going to have a terrible time explaining why I'm arriving at work in such style."

Price grabbed her when she shifted, pulling her onto his lap. He gave her a long, hard kiss, hoping it would encourage her to wrap up her work early. "I'll be here to pick you up at five."

She nodded, her lips puffy from so much kissing. She didn't appear to mind. "Okay. Five."

Gunner chuckled. "Damn. We're seeing a major breakthrough here. Deni's not fighting us for more lab time."

She smirked at Gunner and then cupped Price's cheek in a way that couldn't be described as anything less than genuine affection. No one had ever touched Price that way.

She smiled sadly. "I'll miss you today."

Price swallowed heavily, touched by her admission. "Ditto, beauty."

Roman opened the door and Gunner and Denise got out. Price watched as they walked into the lab, then sighed and rested his head against the seat. The limo had traveled nearly ten blocks before Price realized he was grinning like a damn fool, a lovesick smile plastered on his face.

The Grand Master would have a field day when he found out Price was falling in love with the quirky little scientist.

Time to get his head back in the game. He rarely missed work, so he could only imagine the pile of paperwork he'd have to wade through today. Somehow he'd put Denise and Gunner out of his mind. Eight hours. Surely he could do that.

He glanced at his watch. Or maybe he'd call and talk them into meeting him for lunch. Four hours. Price suspected that was the most he'd be able to manage.

Four hours.

"Listen, I think we could sit here for hours debating the worthiness of—"

Price stopped talking when his personal assistant opened the door of the boardroom and waved to him.

"Yes, Bridget?"

"I'm very sorry to interrupt you, but there's an urgent call on line one."

Price frowned. Bridget knew better than to disrupt a meeting with the stockholders. "Bridget—"

"It's from a Gunner Wells with the FBI. He insisted. Wouldn't take no for an answer."

Price's chest tightened. Denise.

He stood quickly. "If you gentlemen will excuse me."

A couple of men nodded, while he read the curiosity on more than a few faces. No doubt they were dying to know why an FBI agent was calling him with an urgent message. They'd just have to wonder. Price had no answers to give them.

He walked to his office quickly, shut the door, picked up the phone and pressed line one. "Gunner?"

"I know you're in the middle of a big-ass meeting, but you might want to get over here. Curtis has been shot."

"Fuck. Where's Denise?"

"She's fine, but she found him. She's pretty shaken up."

"I'll be right there." Price didn't bother to ask for details. He'd get them once he was sure Denise was okay. He pulled his CFO out of the boardroom and told him he'd have to finish the meeting. Fortunately, he had a good man in place. The CFO simply nodded and said he'd handle it. Then he gave his personal assistant instructions to cancel the rest of his appointments for the day. He called for Roman to meet him in front of the building as he headed for the elevator.

He drummed his fingers on his knee during the return trip to the lab. He'd been an idiot to think the threat against Denise wasn't real. His gut had told him she was in serious danger, but he'd let Denise and that damn FBI agent, Young, convince him it wasn't as bad as he feared.

His heart raced as he considered what this shooting meant. In his rush to get to Denise, he hadn't even asked if poor Curtis was okay. Price hoped so. It was obvious Denise thought the world of the young man. She'd be devastated if he was killed.

He leapt from the limousine as soon as Roman pulled up to the curb, not bothering to wait for his driver to open the door. "Stay close," he instructed the man.

If he felt like there was still a looming danger, he'd hustle Denise out of the building and to his house. He made a mental note to call his butler and inform the man to beef up security around the property.

He was met at the door by a police officer, who started to turn him away.

"It's okay, Officer Riley. I called Price."

The officer stepped aside as Gunner approached. Obviously Gunner had been flashing his FBI credentials around.

Together, they walked toward Denise's office as Gunner quickly filled him in. Apparently, Denise had begun checking her trials as soon as they hit the lab. She'd spent almost an hour going over Curtis's findings and filling Gunner in on her work. Then Gunner had set up his laptop, settling down to work while Denise borrowed his phone to call Curtis, concerned about the man's tardiness.

That was when they heard Curtis's phone ringing in

Denise's office. The door had been closed when they'd arrived and Denise hadn't bothered to open it. When they entered the room, they discovered Curtis lying on Denise's cot, a pool of blood beneath him.

Mercifully, the man was still alive, but barely. No one was exactly sure how much time had passed between the shooting and Denise finding him, but he'd lost a lot of blood.

The ambulance had already left for the hospital, and Gunner said Denise was chomping at the bit to follow. Unfortunately, the lab director and the Boston City Police department had lots of questions for her.

Price paused at the doorway of Denise's lab. She was sitting in a chair, her shoulders slouched, her face pale. He longed to take her in his arms, to hold and console her, but to do so would expose them to too much gossip and supposition. They'd agreed that Gunner would be her boyfriend, Price a benevolent, eccentric friend.

"Deni." Gunner knelt beside her, taking her hand. "Price is here."

Denise looked over and, for a moment, he feared she'd forget her role as her eyes lit up. Gunner must have shared his concern because Price noticed how the other man tightened his grip.

Denise gave him a friendly smile. "It was, um, nice of you to come over."

Price winked covertly and then turned to the police officer questioning her. "I'm Price Bennett," he said, offering his hand to the man.

Then he shook the lab director's hand. The man's eyes widened with recognition and a bit of awe. Price came from one of the oldest families in Boston. The Bennett name was well known in the area as several public buildings were named in honor of various members of his ancestry, including a dorm on campus. "Nice to meet you, Mr. Bennett. Your family's reputation precedes you, as they've provided countless support to our school and facility. I wish we were meeting under better circumstances." Even if the man wondered why Price was there, he had the good grace not to ask. "I need to talk to the security guard on duty last night, make sure he hasn't gone home yet. The police want to question him next. Please excuse me."

Price turned back to the police officer after the lab director left. "Lieutenant Miller?" he asked, glancing at the man's badge.

"That's right. Miller."

While Price didn't want to insult the man, he needed to know the police department could handle this case competently. "I assume you've requested the security surveillance videos? Issued an order to search for the weapon?"

The officer nodded and gestured to Gunner. "He did all that before we arrived." The man's tone let him know he wasn't happy to have to deal with the FBI...and now the CEO of Bennett Securities.

"Very good."

Gunner rose, releasing Denise's hand. "I can tell you now that I suspect the police will find precious little on those videos. There aren't any cameras connected to this corridor and none pointing toward two side entrances. Only the front door is covered."

"Shit," Price muttered.

Gunner raised his hand. "However, the side doors are locked. People can only enter those with a fob, and that information is logged into a computer. I've requested a list of people who used their fobs yesterday and this morning."

"You still don't have any idea when the shooting actually occurred?" Price asked.

Gunner shook his head. "The nearest the EMT could guess was somewhere after two a.m. Maybe the doctors at the hospital can give us a better estimate."

Denise looked at him, tears brimming in the corners of her eyes. "The EMT said if we hadn't found him when we did, he would have died from blood loss."

Price couldn't stand it anymore. Trinity Masters be damned. He walked over and helped her stand, wrapping her in a tight embrace. "I'm so sorry, Denise."

Lieutenant Miller cleared his throat. "Agent Wells said that Dr. Parker's apartment was broken into a few nights ago?"

Price released Denise but kept his hand on her back, offering her support. "That's right."

"And there was a bomb recovered from the scene?"

Denise sighed. "I've already told you all this. Can I please go to the hospital?"

The police officer looked from Gunner to Price. Price could read the confusion and frustration in his eyes. Obviously he was struggling to figure out the group dynamics of the three people in the room and he suspected they knew more than they were saying.

"If you discover you have any more questions for Denise, you can reach her at my place." Price handed the man his business card.

"So, what are you?" Lieutenant Miller asked. "Her bodyguard?"

Gunner nodded. "That's exactly what he is. I hired him. Mr. Bennett has been kind enough to offer the use of his guesthouse to Deni and I until we find out who's trying to harm her. Now if you'll excuse us."

Gunner wrapped his arm about Denise's waist, holding her close enough to leave no doubt of his romantic relationship with the pretty scientist. Price walked two steps ahead of them, assuming his role as bodyguard. Gunner had told the lie smoothly. Price appreciated his friend's steady nerves.

Typically Price was better at shielding his emotions, but he'd been thrown for a loop ever since Denise's sweet farewell kiss in the limo this morning. Though in all fairness, Gunner had had years to accept his feelings for Denise. They were still too new, too unexpected for Price.

Price helped Denise into the car, followed Gunner in and then instructed Roman to take them to the hospital.

Denise turned to look out the window as the car started moving. Unwilling to keep up the distance between them, he moved closer, placing his arms around her shoulders.

Denise was still for several seconds and then she shifted, wrapping her arm around his waist as she pressed her head against his chest. "That bullet was meant for me."

Price knew her words were true, but he couldn't let her carry around that kind of guilt. "You don't know that, Denise."

She lifted her head, her face only inches from his. Misery was written in her eyes. "Yes, I do. Curtis never sleeps in the lab office, and everyone knows it. It would have been me on that cot, if…"

Her words drifted away. She didn't have to finish. They all knew where she'd been. Why Curtis had been sleeping at the lab.

"He's going to be okay, Deni." Gunner shifted from the side couch, claiming the spot on her other side. He rested his hand on her knee. "You have to keep faith."

"Why would someone want to kill me? Is what I'm doing really so bad? I just want to help people. Find a way for them to live without pain, without losing their memories or their minds."

Gunner grasped her hand. "You're not doing anything wrong. The only villain in this is the person tormenting you."

"My dad had early onset Alzheimer's. Did I ever tell you that?"

Gunner shook his head. "You've never mentioned your dad."

"My parents had me later in life, both of them were thirty-eight when I was born. I don't know if they intended to have any more kids, but when my dad was forty, he was diagnosed with Alzheimer's."

"I didn't realize someone so young could get Alzheimer's." Price hated the desolate look in Denise's eyes.

"It's rare, but it happens. My dad fought it for a few years, but it got bad. He couldn't remember who I was most days, but every now and then, there would be this moment of clarity. And it was good. We'd talk and it was nice."

Price started doing the math. Denise couldn't have been more than six years old. How much had watching her father's suffering impacted her, driven her decisions in life? Given her present profession, her non-stop working and determination to succeed, he'd say those early years had changed everything for her.

"What happened to your dad, Deni?"

Denise didn't look at Gunner—or at him—as she responded. Instead, she gazed straight ahead. "During one of his lucid periods, he killed himself. He always said he didn't want to be a bother to my mother, didn't want me to remember him as some lost soul. So he ended it."

Price felt as if he'd been punched in the stomach. "How old were you?"

"Seven."

"Jesus." Gunner's muttered comment mirrored Price's thoughts.

"It's okay," she said after a few moments. "I've made my peace with it. I really have. He wanted to die with dignity. That was his choice to make. I just want a world where no one else has to make that same decision."

Price took her hand and squeezed it. Game over. He was in love with this woman and he would be until the day he died.

"We're here," Gunner said as they pulled up to the hospital. They spent several hours sitting in the emergency room waiting for Curtis to come out of surgery, then even longer as the staff delivered him to recovery.

Denise held herself together until the doctor assured them Curtis was out of danger. Then she fell apart, crying tears of relief as Gunner held her.

They walked to Curtis's room together, allowing Denise to introduce them. She called Gunner her boyfriend and explained Price was a friend. Curtis accepted the news that she had a boyfriend with wide eyes and a loud hoot. Price instantly liked the research assistant.

When Gunner asked if he had seen his shooter. Curtis shook his head. He said that one minute he felt a sharp pain, the next he was waking up in this room.

Gunner and Price said their goodbyes and then stood outside the door of Curtis's hospital room while Denise visited a little longer.

After ten minutes, she emerged. "He's asleep."

Gunner took her hand as they returned to the limo. It was early evening. The sun was just dipping below the horizon, painting the sky a muted orange. Price's house was on the outskirts of the city and the ride there was spent in quiet contemplation. None of them broke the silence, all of them lost in their own thoughts.

It had been a long, stressful day, and all Price could think about was getting something to eat and settling down in front of the fireplace to relax with Gunner and Denise. He'd called ahead to let his cook know when they would arrive. After the meal, he'd send the servants to their living quarters. He wanted to show Gunner and Denise around their new home without the presence of others.

When they drove through the gated entrance, Denise gasped quietly as Gunner muttered, "holy fuck."

He'd grown up in the large mansion in Watertown, but even Price could appreciate the majesty of it. He hoped they wouldn't find it too intimidating or overwhelming.

"You really live here?" Denise asked. "Alone?"

Price took her hand as they exited the limo and led her up the grand staircase to the front door. "I do. I moved out after graduation and spent a few years in an apartment in downtown Boston. When my parents passed away, it seemed wrong not to move back home."

"It's beautiful." Denise's eyes widened when they stepped into the elegant foyer. His butler and housekeeper were there to greet them.

"Good evening, Mr. Bennett. Beverly has dinner ready for you as requested. I'll help Roman carry in the bags. Joyce has prepared the guest rooms in the left wing.

Price shook his head. "No, put their bags in the right wing, in the room next to mine." The right wing had always been reserved for family only, the left used to accommodate out of town guests.

His butler, Patrick, nodded his head, hiding his surprise much better than Joyce, who began to eye Denise and Gunner with genuine curiosity.

Most of the servants in the house had worked for the Bennett family for decades. Price knew their loyalty was unwavering and his trust in them was absolute. While they might be able to hide their true association from the rest of the world, it would be impossible to do so at home.

Sometime soon, he would have to pull Joyce and Patrick

aside, explain that he would be living in a ménage relationship and make sure they understood the importance of their silence.

He wasn't looking forward to that awkward conversation.

Price led them to the dining room and they took their seats at one end of the long tiger-wood table. The silence from the limo drifted to the house, making dinner a tense affair. Price missed the casual conversations that had taken place around the tiny table in the hotel. Finally, he couldn't take it anymore. Price pushed away the coconut-crème pie his cook had made for dessert. "So what do you think of the place?"

Denise put down her fork, glancing around at the ornate dining room. He should have told the serving staff to set the meal up at the kitchen table. He only used this room when entertaining.

"I'm afraid to touch anything," she confessed.

Gunner nodded. "It's like living in a museum."

Price had done a terrible job introducing them to his home. So far he'd shown them the front foyer and the dining room, both places he rarely inhabited.

"Come on. Time for you to see the rest of the house."

He led them toward the back of the house, past all the public rooms. He'd show them the parlor and living room tomorrow. Tonight, they needed to see that despite the size of the mansion, it was truly a home.

They stepped into the family room and Denise released a long sigh of relief. He'd redecorated the room when he took over the house, making it a comfortable place where he could come home, kick off his shoes and recline in front of the TV for a few hours before bed.

"Now this is what I'm talking about." Gunner dropped down in one of the recliners, tugging on the pulley until it slid back and the foot cushion rose. "Oh yeah. This is good."

Price chuckled. "Glad you like my chair."

Denise kicked off her shoes and sat down on the plush couch. "I love this room."

"Good. Because I suspect this is where we'll spend most of our evenings together. The kitchen is through there with a breakfast nook. That's where I eat my meals when I'm not entertaining. My home office is through that door, but it's large enough that I suspect we could set up two more desks, so each of us has our own workspace."

"And we'll sleep in the right wing?" Denise asked.

He nodded, wishing she didn't still look quite so overwhelmed.

"I haven't been in the left wing in nearly three months. It's shut up most of the time, only opened when someone comes to visit. I promise you, the family wing is just as homey and comfortable as this room. If you can forget about the extra, overdone, under-used rooms, I promise you this house is just as laid-back as the next place. What's mine is yours, and I'm hoping you'll want to add your own stuff, your own touches. This is our home now. If you want it to be. If not..."

He wasn't sure what else to say. He loved his home and he wanted them to stay. But if they weren't comfortable moving in, he would pack up and follow where they led. He didn't have a choice. Not because of his vow to the Trinity Masters, but because of the commitment he felt toward them.

"I like it here." Denise lifted her feet beneath her and collapsed against the back of the couch. "It's your home. I'm touched that you want to share it with us."

He grinned. Leave it to Denise to know exactly the right thing to say. He joined her on the couch. "I'm glad you're here."

He reached out to touch her hair, and just like that the atmosphere in the room became charged, electric. Gunner didn't move from the recliner, but Price could feel his eyes on them, watching as Price leaned closer to kiss her.

Price wasted no time advancing their play. He reached for Denise's breasts, rubbing them through the material of her blouse and bra. She twisted on the couch until she faced him.

"Take off her shirt," Gunner directed.

Price glanced over at the recliner. Gunner had lowered the footrest and leaned forward, but he didn't come to join them.

"I want to watch you fuck our girl," Gunner said as he reached for the button at his waistband, unfastening it before sliding down the zipper. Then he lifted his hips just enough to shove his pants and boxers to his knees. His cock stood erect, the head brushing against his stomach. Gunner gripped himself tightly, then lifted his head and gestured for Price to keep going.

Their lover was a voyeur. Price had never considered himself an exhibitionist, but knowing that Gunner was watching drove even more blood to his cock.

Price reached for Denise's blouse. He started to unfasten the first button but then decided he didn't have time for that. He ripped the material along the front, dragging it over her arms. Her bra quickly followed.

Price laid her down on the couch, caging her beneath him as he roughly sucked first one and then the other nipple into his mouth.

Denise gripped his hair with her fingers and he sensed she was torn between holding him to her and pushing him away. She was new to pleasurable pain. When she moaned, pulling him closer, he resisted the urge to pump a fist in the air. She would accept everything they dished out. During their time at the hotel they'd limited their sex play, keeping it as vanilla as a threesome could. He and Gunner took turns fucking her, teaching her how to suck their cocks.

Now, Price longed to expand on those lessons. He wanted to spank her, tie her up, blindfold her, fuck her ass. A lifetime wouldn't be long enough to explore all the ways he wanted to take her.

"Get those fucking pants off her," Gunner demanded.

Price heard Gunner's quiet panting, could see his friend stroking his own cock as he watched them.

Price tackled the zipper on Denise's slacks, stripping them and her panties away. Then he released himself from the confinement of his pants. He restrained a groan of relief as the pressure of the thick material on his cock was lifted. He quickly shed his shirt as well.

"Fuck her with your fingers. I want to hear her cry out, wanna watch her close those pretty blue eyes of hers when she comes."

Price wanted the same thing. He dragged his fingers along her wet slit, toying with her clit. Denise lifted her hips when he pinched it.

"Oh, God," she muttered, her head thrashing on the cushions. "Please."

Price grinned. "That's right, beauty. Beg me. Beg for it."

"Price." She fisted her hands into the couch cushions as he pressed two fingers deep inside her. He didn't give her time to adjust to the invasion. Instead, he released the reins, gave in to the need driving him. He prided himself on his control. His finesse. His skills in the bedroom.

Denise stripped that pride away.

He thrust his fingers deep, driving her quickly to climax. She screamed as she came. Price continued to take, demanded more. He added a third finger and pressed his thumb against her clit. She stiffened and came again.

"God dammit, Price. Fuck her. Fuck her hard."

A quick glance to his left confirmed Gunner was close. His hand was slapping his flesh faster.

Price pulled out his fingers and replaced them with his

dick. He shoved in to the hilt as Denise lifted her hands to his upper arms. She dug into the flesh there, scraping her nails over his skin. He relished the pain.

Over and over, he pounded into her until her sex clenched, her orgasm forcing him to fall off the cliff as well.

Jets of come erupted, and still he thrust, moving until every last drop was squeezed out.

When he opened his eyes, regained his senses, Gunner was there, standing next to them. Price couldn't look away as Gunner stroked his own cock harder, faster.

Denise lay still beneath them, and then she reached down to cup her breasts, holding them up, offering them. "Come on me," she pleaded.

Her words claimed another causality. Gunner's free hand flew to Price's shoulder, clinging to him for support as he climaxed, his come covering Denise's breasts, her stomach.

It was the hottest thing Price had ever seen.

Neither of them moved for a few minutes, then Gunner pulled away and dragged his pants up without bothering to refasten them.

"How many rooms are in this house, Price?" he asked.

Price shrugged. "Christ. I don't know. Dozens."

Gunner grinned at him, slapping Price on the back. "Well, we just initiated the first one. What do you say we tackle the shower next?"

CHAPTER SIX

Gunner walked into Price's office early the next morning and dropped a folder in front of him.

Price looked up from his computer screen. "What's this?"

"Read it."

Price opened the file and began to scan it. His expression grew darker. Twice, he mumbled the word, "fuck," but he continued reading the information.

Finally, he looked up. "Where did you get this?"

Gunner gave him a crooked grin but didn't bother to reply.

"It would appear the Reverend is a bit more dangerous than your friend at the FBI led us to believe."

Gunner shrugged. "The FBI isn't exactly known for offering full disclosure. Young wasn't going to share all the details with you and Deni."

"But he was willing to give you this dossier?"

"He was. I think it's safe to say Deni has caught the attention of a psychopath. Our inside source says the man's sermons are almost exclusively focused on stem-cell research these days, and how it's murder and the prelude to some doomsday end-times. Prior to his run-in with Deni at the library, he seemed inclined to spread his venom around to multiple groups—condemning abortion clinics, homosexuals, as well as other misguided souls." Gunner put air quotes around the word misguided. "The man genuinely believes he's a prophet sent here to clean house. If he fails, he promises hellfire, damnation and basically everything else mentioned in the book of Revelations."

"So he's the precursor to the four horsemen of the apocalypse?"

Gunner nodded. "Something like that."

"What I don't understand is how this man has found so many followers who will buy into this bullshit. According to your file on him, he's acquired quite a bit of wealth from the generous donations of his congregation."

"People are afraid these days. Turn on the news, for God's sake. Between what's happening in the Middle East and new, deadly diseases being found every day, folks are in panic mode. They're afraid of dying, and the good Reverend is offering to sell them salvation. Clear out the riff-raff and all will be well. Get rid of the baby killers and homosexuals and we'll buy ourselves a few thousand more years on the planet." Gunner leaned against Price's desk. "The Reverend is a gifted speaker with the ability to read people's fears. He preys on that."

"And he's determined that Denise is public enemy number one?"

Gunner frowned. "It would appear so. Apparently she engaged with him in a mini-debate at the end of her talk at the library. He'd come to protest and Deni actually thought she could make a crazy man see reason. My source says the Reverend has held up a picture of Deni at their religious gatherings, called her the daughter of Satan. It's like he's gathering a lynch mob. Scary shit."

"I don't like this." Price slammed his hand on the file. "Dammit. This man has to be stopped."

"Agreed, but he hasn't technically done anything wrong. Deni could probably slap him with a slander suit, but that would only fuel the fire."

"The man has to be doing something illegal that we could have him arrested for."

Gunner sighed. "If there is, law enforcement hasn't found it yet. The Reverend's been on their radar for a little over a year now. The man pays taxes, files the proper paperwork for his gatherings, and he's entitled to freedom of speech under the Constitution."

"What about the crimes Young said he'd committed? The arson, vandalism?"

"The Reverend already had his day in court. Paid his fines, served a few nights in the local jail, then he returned to the pulpit and quoted scripture about the persecution prophets of the past had suffered at the hands of an unjust government and blind sinners."

"I don't like this."

Gunner agreed. "My source says the Reverend's become more manic in the past few months, more outspoken, outwardly agitated and aggressive. He truly seems to believe the end is near and he's running out of time. His followers have picked up on that and they're in panic mode as well."

Price rubbed his forehead wearily. Gunner knew he hadn't slept well the night before. After their interlude in the living room, they'd climbed the stairs and dropped into Price's big bed. While Deni had slept soundly, he and Price had done more than their fair share of tossing and turning. He suspected neither of them would rest easy until Deni was out of danger.

"Do you think some of these followers are freaking out enough to kill?"

Gunner's chest tightened. "Yeah. I do. Someone shot Curtis and I'm pretty damn sure he wasn't the intended target. Whether it was the Reverend or one of his believers remains to be seen. Given the information we've uncovered so far, I've called my boss in D.C. and requested that I be allowed to stay in Boston to work on this case. Incredibly enough, he agreed. I thought I was going to have to put up more of a fight."

Price's smug face told Gunner he wasn't surprised by the news he was staying in Boston.

Gunner narrowed his eyes. "Looks like I'm not the only person privy to insider information. One of these days, you're going to have to explain to me how a person works their way up the ranks of the Trinity Masters' organization."

Price turned away and reached behind him for a magazine. "That saying is still in effect even if the FBI didn't coin it. Tell you, kill you. I was actually on my way to find you and Denise when you brought in that file." Price tossed a copy of The Bostonian, a local magazine on top of the dossier about the Reverend. "Denise appears to be her own worst enemy right now."

The magazine showed a smiling Deni standing at the counter in her lab, surrounded by test tubes, Petri dishes and a large microscope. The headline read Scientist Making a Miracle?

Gunner closed his eyes and sighed. "Great. Why doesn't she wave a red flag in front of the bull?"

Price nodded. "She's definitely thrown gasoline on a wildfire. What are we going to do?"

Gunner had spent most of the morning asking himself that same question. "I'd like to tie her to the bed and keep her there until the threat is gone—preferably nude."

Price laughed. "I like your thinking, but I'm fairly sure that's not going to fly with our little bride. She's bound and determined to continue her research."

"I know. I suspect the police will lock down her lab for a few days since it's a crime scene, so that could help us keep her out of the public eye for a little while."

"Maybe we could stretch the truth on how long their investigation is taking."

Gunner frowned. "Are you suggesting we lie to her?"

"No. Not really. I mean...yeah, maybe. Dammit." Price ran a hand through his hair, his frustration growing. "I want her safe, Gunner."

"I understand that. I do too. But I'm not sure I'm comfortable lying to her. It feels like a bad way to start this..." His words drifted away as he tried to figure out what to call this.

Gunner realized Price and Deni had done the same thing he had. They'd eschewed normal relationships, content to let the Trinity Masters determine their path. As a result, the three of them were struggling with the basics involved in making a commitment to someone.

"Until we decide about that, I'd rather not tell her what we know about the Reverend. She's still upset about Curtis. I don't want to scare her. Maybe we could find some way to stress to her how important it is that she not put herself in harm's way. I'm going to encourage her to move her research here."

Gunner nodded. "That would certainly make her easier to protect, but I'm not sure she'll go for it."

"Hey. What are you guys up to?" Deni walked into the office.

Gunner grinned, wondering when the sight of a woman in SpongeBob pajama bottoms, a T-shirt that said "Black Holes Suck" and a messy ponytail started inspiring instant lust in him.

"We were looking at this." Price handed Deni his copy of The Bostonian.

"Oh, hey, I forgot about that interview. Crap. I hate that picture of me." Deni turned her nose up at the sight of her smiling face on the cover.

Price shook his head. "I think you're missing the point, Denise. We're trying to lay low until the threat against you is removed. Plastering your picture all over a popular local magazine isn't particularly smart."

Deni frowned. "First of all, I did that interview a couple months ago. It was actually my lecture at the library and the run-in with the Reverend that caught the reporter's attention."

"Great," Price muttered.

"Did you read the article?" she asked.

Gunner shook his head, but from the scowl on Price's face, he could tell the other man had read it.

"The reporter asked me about the protestors."

Gunner knew he wasn't going to like what was coming next. "And you said?"

"I may have made some comment about people protesting without getting all the facts. That a lot of their complaints weren't accurate."

Price crossed his arms. "I recall reading something about ignorance playing a role as well."

Deni looked chagrined. "I was still pissed off at the Reverend at the time."

Gunner rubbed his temple. "Jesus, Deni."

"It honestly slipped my mind given all the stuff that's been going on lately. Now I realize I should have remembered, should have asked the magazine to pull the story."

Gunner put his arm around her shoulders and tugged her closer. "It's okay. I think we can all agree it's been a crazy few days. We're just worried this article is going to stir the pot. It could make things even more dangerous for you."

"Yeah. I know. And I'm sorry. I understand you're both worried and I promise I will be very careful. I just got off the phone with the lab director and he's put the building on lockdown until the police catch whoever shot Curtis. It'll be so much safer now than—"

Price pounded his fist on the desk as he stood. "Dammit, Denise. You're not going back to work."

"So I'm under house arrest? A captive again?"

Price's voice was loud, angry. "If that's how you want to look at it. I have no problem with that. I'll do whatever is necessary to keep you safe."

Gunner closed his eyes and prepared for the inevitable. Somehow he'd need to instruct Price on the concept of catching flies with honey rather than vinegar.

Deni's back stiffened, her eyes narrowing with anger. "Keep me safe? Screw that. There's no way I'm spending the rest of my life swaddled in bubble wrap just for your peace of mind. I told you both that I have to go back to—"

"Deni, you're not going to be able to return to your lab for a few days. The police have it cordoned off as a crime scene. I doubt they'll allow you in right away." Gunner hoped his calm logic would work.

"I know that. I was going to see if they would let me move some of my things to the lab next to mine. I'm good friends with Dr. Madigan and I'm sure he wouldn't mind if—"

"They won't let you take anything out of the lab."

Deni walked to the desk and sat down in Price's chair. Gunner hated the defeated look on her face.

"I need to get in there."

Gunner knelt in front of her. "I know that. What if I talk to the police and see if they'll allow me to transport some of your stuff here? You could give me a list of what you need—"

Deni shook her head. "Some of my samples are fragile. This isn't like packing up books and dishes. It would be better if I could work at the lab."

Price turned away from them, walking to the window. "You can't."

"I told you—"

Price whirled on her. "I know what you said, but it's simply too dangerous."

Deni sighed. "Then he's won."

Gunner stood up but remained close to her. "Who's won?"

She looked down at her hands, clenching them together. "Whoever is after me. A lot of my work is time sensitive. If I stop now, I may as well throw up the white flag and surrender. It will set me back years. Without Curtis there to keep things rolling..." Her words drifted away.

Gunner pulled his cell phone out of his pocket. "Let me make a few calls. I don't want to rush things though. Price is right. The danger surrounding you is very real. Can you give me two days to figure out an answer, a way to get you to your research or vice versa?"

Deni jumped up and hugged him. "Yes. Two days will be fine. I actually have some data I can sort through until then. My lab director is sending someone over with a loaner laptop. He was able to download most of my current research to a flash drive."

Deni walked away from them and it was obvious her mind was already at work as she began to clear away some books and magazines from a side table. "I can set up here if it won't bother you, Price."

Price approached her, shaking his head. "You aren't going to spend the next two days working, Denise."

"But Gunner said—"

"Gunner said he needed two days to sort things out. He said nothing about you using that time to work. Personally, I think there are more important things for us to test out, experiment with."

Gunner chuckled. Their time in the hotel had been far too brief for him. And while he knew perfectly well they were still in the honeymoon phase and that eventually they'd hit some brick walls they would have to scale, for now he intended to bask in the insatiable lust he felt whenever the three of them were together. Besides, they hadn't touched the tip of the iceberg on all the sexual activities he planned to explore. "I'd be on board for that."

Deni frowned. "I have no idea what you're talking about."

Price grasped Deni's hand and lifted it to his lips. "I thought perhaps we could expand on that house-arrest idea. I enjoyed holding you captive at the hotel."

Gunner stepped closer, pressing Deni between him and Price, letting the feeling of being trapped sink in. "You looked hot as hell in my handcuffs."

Deni shivered. "There are servants around."

Price shook his head. "No. I gave them all the day off. The house is empty. Our own mansion playground. Do you still want to escape?"

Deni looked over her shoulder at Gunner. Her face was flushed and he spotted the interest and the mischief in her eyes. "Do you two really think you can hold me?"

A dare. A fucking sexy one. Gunner's cock went from mildly interested to fuck her now in an instant. "I don't think there's any question about that." He was no slouch at sexual threats either.

Deni shook her head, her eyes becoming sad. It took Gunner unaware. He stepped back. "Deni?"

Price recognized the change as well. He released her hand. "Are you okay?"

She nodded slowly. "Yeah. I just can't stop thinking about what suckers you guys both are." Before she finished speaking, she'd taken advantage of the distance they'd provided and sprinted for the office door. "Catch me if you can," she yelled over her shoulder before slamming the door behind her and disappearing from view.

Price burst out laughing but lost no time in chasing her.

Gunner heard Price's surprised, "Where the hell did she go?" when he threw open the door.

Gunner chuckled and then decided it would take more than mere speed to catch her. They'd have to be sneaky.

He exited the office by a second door, intending to trap her. He circled around the house in the opposite direction of Price. Perhaps they could corner her. When he and Price met in the middle, it was apparent their little scientist was a master at hide and seek. They continued along their original paths, away from each other. Gunner slowed his pace, searching for places where she might hide and listening for her footsteps.

A creak sounded in the dining room. Price must have heard it too because suddenly he was standing behind him, silently pointing to another door. Because of the sheer size of the house, most rooms had two means of entry. Price took off for the kitchen, intent on entering from that angle, while Gunner covered the entrance from the foyer. They approached silently. Gunner was impressed by Price's stealth. For a large man, Price was a master at sneaking around covertly. It dawned on Gunner that Price would make an excellent FBI agent.

Peering in the doorway, he spotted Price entering across the room. He stepped into the dining room as well, but at first glance he found no sign of Deni. Then his gaze landed on the table. An ornate tablecloth that reached to the floor covered it.

It appeared to be slightly askew. In a normal home, Gunner wouldn't have noticed, but Price's servants kept an immaculate house. He pointed to the table and Price nodded.

Each of them took an end of the long rectangular table, but before they could lift the cloth, Deni darted out from the side, knocking over a chair in the process. She tried to pass him, but he was ready for her. Gunner grabbed her as she squealed with laughter. Price joined them, capturing Deni's flailing arms and pressing them against her back as Gunner pinned her against him by gripping her waist tightly.

"Ready to cry uncle?" Price asked.

Deni shook her head and continued to struggle, though it was obvious she was outnumbered.

"Cry uncle now and we'll lighten your punishment. Go easy on you."

Deni stilled. "Punishment?" There was no mistaking the breathless excitement in her tone.

Gunner tugged her closer, let her feel his hard cock against her stomach. "Forget it. Offer's rescinded."

Price held Deni's arms behind her as Gunner untied the string holding her pajama pants up. Deni stopped fighting. Her breasts were thrust out from Price's capture, rising and falling rapidly as she tried to catch her breath from the chase. Gunner couldn't look away. Her nipples were tight and poking through the thin material of her T-shirt. He imagined what they would look like with nipple clamps.

Impatient for more, Gunner roughly shoved her pants and panties over her hips, past her knees. "Kick them off."

She obeyed, bare from the waist down in seconds.

Gunner was torn between asking Price to release her so they could strip off her shirt and having him grip her tighter. He wasn't sure why he found the image of her confinement so arousing.

Price took the decision from him. "Lift that tablecloth and push the dishes and utensils toward the middle."

Gunner grinned, understanding exactly what Price wanted. He bared a spot on the table and Price pushed Deni over the surface. She shivered. Arousal? A chill caused by the cool wood? It didn't matter. Gunner intended to warm her up soon enough.

Price kept his grip tight against Deni's wrists. "You were a bad girl, Denise."

She shook her head, but Gunner couldn't tell if she was denying his words or trying to ward off her needs.

Gunner pushed her legs apart and pressed two fingers deep inside her. She was on fire, drenched. Their woman loved the thrill of the chase. Good.

Because Gunner would want to do this again. And again.

He thrust his fingers in and out several times until Deni moaned, lifting her hips in silent invitation for more. Then he withdrew. "Nope. No reward for you. This is punishment, remember?"

Deni closed her eyes and pressed her forehead against the smooth surface of the table. "Please," she begged.

Price shifted, holding both her hands with one of his. With his free hand, he swatted her ass. It was a light blow. Deni jerked, but Gunner knew it was surprise, not pain that prompted her response.

"Do that again."

Gunner grinned at her request and complied. Unlike Price, he added a bit of force to the motion.

She groaned but didn't try to escape. "Again."

Price answered her call this time. They took turns spanking her as Deni started to squirm on the table, her body overheated, looking for satisfaction.

Price thrust three fingers inside her pussy, and Deni cried

out. Price still held her wrists tightly, the captivity obviously driving her arousal higher.

"More," she demanded.

Gunner reached toward her sex and his gaze locked with Price's. The man nodded in silent understanding. Price removed two of his fingers, allowing Gunner to enter her body as well. Their knuckles rubbed together as each of them pressed a finger deep into her. Deni's cries encouraged them to push harder, faster.

Gunner was surprised when Price pulled his finger out. Then, as Gunner watched, Price pressed his wet digit against her anus. Deni's thrashing stilled, but she didn't try to get away.

"Yes," she hissed.

Price entered her, his finger slowly moving in past the first knuckle, then the second. Gunner withdrew, returning to her pussy with three fingers. He stroked her slowly as Price continued to press into her ass.

When Price was fully lodged, they all froze, the moment charged with electricity, heat, desire. Then they moved, taking both her holes at the same time.

Her orgasm came hard, her inner muscles clenching tightly. Gunner felt lightheaded as he recalled how amazing her climax felt against his cock. His jeans were too tight, cutting into his dick until he was in true physical pain. He couldn't wait another second longer.

"Upstairs," Gunner said, his voice husky, hungry.

He expected Price to agree. Instead, Price shook his head and released his grip on Deni's hands. He helped her stand, supporting her with his undeniable strength. Gunner had always considered himself well built, but that was before he'd come face-to-face with Price Bennett. Price would give the Mr. Universe contenders a run for their money.

"Deni," Price started. "If we go upstairs now, this experiment continues."

Deni nodded slowly, but Price wasn't appeased.

"Do you understand what I'm saying? I want to take your ass while Gunner fucks your pussy."

Deni winced slightly. No doubt she found Price's words crude. It didn't matter. Gunner appreciated his friend's blunt honesty.

Gunner cupped her cheek. "Will you take us both?"

She bit her lower lip and, for a painfully long moment, it felt as if all the air had been sucked out of the room. Then she said, "Yes."

Her agreement released Price's restraint. He lifted her and carried her upstairs to his bedroom as Gunner followed, his head whirling over what they were about to do. Christ. Sometimes it was hard to recall they'd only been together in this triad a few days. So much had happened. It felt like they were constantly moving in fast-forward.

Except for the times when they came together like this. Then time slowed down as they escaped the world, the worries at work, the threat to Deni, the craziness of this relationship. In moments like these, everything just clicked.

Price carried Deni to the bed. He placed her on her feet and quickly stripped off her shirt. Then he gestured for her to crawl onto the mattress. Deni took her place in the middle. One night in this bed and they'd already claimed sides, pillows.

He and Price both undressed before joining her.

Gunner reached for her, pulled her in his arms and kissed her. He was aware of Price moving around behind them, the sound of a drawer opening and closing, but he was too wrapped up in Deni's soft lips, her sweet taste, her hot breath on his face, to care what Price was doing.

They parted when Price rolled closer, tugging Deni away from him. "Get in the middle, Gunner. On your back."

Gunner didn't mind taking directions from Price. He'd noticed several times that they'd fallen into a tacit agreement. Sometimes Price took the lead, other times Gunner did. There was no contest between them. Just the give and take required to make a relationship like this work.

Gunner moved into position as Price instructed Deni to straddle him. Deni lifted her leg, kneeling over Gunner on her hands and knees. His cock was hard, lying on his stomach. He reached down to grip it, pushing it up. "Come here, Deni. I want to be inside you."

She smiled, lifting her hips and sinking down so slowly Gunner saw stars. Her innocence was truly gone, and left in its place was a passionate woman with needs that were almost as primal as his. There was no denying or refusing them.

When she was fully seated, Gunner gripped her hips firmly and held her in place.

"Lean forward." Price gently pressed on Deni's upper back until she lay atop Gunner. Her nipples rubbed against his chest until Gunner couldn't resist giving them a quick squeeze. Deni's eyes glazed with desire as he lightly pinched her nipples.

"Raise your hands above your head, Denise."

Both Deni and Gunner glanced up as Price captured her wrists once more, securing them to the middle of his headboard with straps Gunner hadn't noticed the night before.

"Your captivity isn't over yet." Price's dark threat caused Deni to shiver.

Gunner tightened his grip on her breasts. "You're ours."

The room fell silent as Price took his place behind Deni. Like her, he straddled Gunner's legs, allowing him to feel the heavy weight of Price's balls on his shins. He'd never been attracted to a man, never truly let himself imagine being in bed with another man, even though he knew it was a distinct possibility when he joined the Trinity Masters. However, Price's nudity and his actions fueled Gunner's arousal even more. He wondered if their sexual exploration would stop with the things they could do with Deni or if—eventually—somewhere down the road, this ménage would evolve into even more. Gunner would have sworn at the introduction ceremony hell would freeze over before he'd consider that. Now he wasn't so sure.

Gunner watched as Price flipped the cap on a tube of lubrication. He pressed the nozzle to Deni's ass. She started to lift up, but Gunner wrapped his arms around her waist, holding her in place. She wouldn't have been able to escape anyway given the ties on her wrists, but he understood the effect Price was aiming for.

They both longed to capture, to possess their precious wife, bind her to them in ways she'd never imagined existed.

Deni groaned as Price worked his fingers into her ass. Gunner's cock was still buried deep inside her and he could feel the other man's progress. Jesus. He could feel it.

For several painfully arousing minutes, Price stretched her, allowing her ample time to become accustomed to the invasion while adding more and more lube. Finally, he withdrew and replaced his fingers with his cock.

Time stood still as Price slowly drove his erection in. Gunner suspected neither he nor Deni took a breath as Price went deeper.

When he was fully lodged, Gunner sucked in some much needed air. "Breathe, Deni."

She lifted her head from where it lay on his chest and looked at him. "Wow," she whispered.

Gunner chuckled. "You can say that again."

"Does it hurt, Denise?"

She shook her head. "A little, but not too much. I like it."

Price withdrew a fraction of an inch and then thrust back, adding some force to his action. Deni gasped.

"You still like it?"

She nodded, so Price continued to up the ante, pulling out farther on each retreat, coming back in harder, deeper.

Gunner picked up the pace, lifting Deni's hips, moving her on his cock in time with Price's fucking. Gunner had never felt anything so incredible.

The thin wall of tissue inside her that separated his cock from Price's dick seemed non-existent, and Gunner felt like he was the one being fucked by two lovers.

The silence in the room was filled by their quiet groans and the sounds of their flesh slapping against each other. Sweat trickled along Gunner's cheek. Deni's skin grew damp as well, making it harder for him to hold on to her. Soon passion overrode everything, and their motions became erratic as each of them reached for their climax.

Deni came loudly, her clenching pussy shoving Gunner over as well. Price was two heartbeats behind them and they tumbled together.

When Gunner opened his eyes, he realized Price was no longer inside Deni's ass. Price released the straps and then tugged Deni's boneless form to the side. Gunner caught Price's gaze and the other man smiled.

"Can't decide if she fell asleep or passed out," Price whispered.

Gunner grinned. Deni's head still rested on his shoulder as Price spooned her from behind. It was midday, but neither of them bothered to rise.

Gunner recalled Price's admission about participating in ménage sex. "Have you ever done that before?"

Price shook his head. "No. It felt like..." Price's words faded.

Gunner understood. "Like we were fucking each other as well as her."

Price studied Gunner's face and then nodded. "It was good."

They lay in silence for several minutes, the two of them simply looking at each other across Deni's body.

Finally, Gunner said, "It was really good."

Price grinned and they both closed their eyes. There was still so much to figure out, to uncover, to enjoy.

Gunner couldn't wait.

CHAPTER SEVEN

Deni looked out the window, staring at Price's beautifully landscaped front yard and watched the sun rise on her fifth day at the mansion. She hadn't left the place since Price brought her and Gunner here from the hospital. Gunner said her lab was still under the control of the Boston Police Department and no amount of flashing his FBI credentials or yelling on his part was going to get her back in, but there was a part of her that wasn't sure she completely believed that.

She called Curtis every day to check on him. She'd asked to visit him a couple times, but whenever she made the suggestion, Price and Gunner had seduced her until she forgot everything...including her own name.

She'd spent the first few days lost in a haze of non-stop sex. Years of abstinence had been put to rest by nights—and days—of endless craving...and indulging. She'd fallen under Price and Gunner's spell, her addiction to their touches, their kisses, too powerful to resist.

Today, she'd shaken herself free of the enchantment. The

hourglass had precious few bits of sand left to fall and she really needed to go back to work. She hadn't exaggerated the time sensitivity of her research. It was time she broke the chains of their sexual captivity.

Her gaze fell on her car. Price's driver had gone to pick it up from the lab and bring it back here the day before yesterday. Roman had handed her the keys upon his return and she'd put them in her messenger bag.

The three of them had stayed up late last night, reaching out for each other even though their bodies had been pushed to the limit of sheer exhaustion. Now it was early and she suspected they'd sleep several more hours.

Good. It was time to take control of her life back. She'd spoken to the lab director every day and he'd assured her nothing else amiss had occurred. Obviously the lockdown was working.

Deni grabbed her purse and jacket and quietly let herself out of the house after disengaging the lock on the front gate. She pressed a button and watched it swing open. Freedom was within her grasp.

Hopefully she'd get a few hours of work in before her overprotective lovers discovered her missing. If she could prove to them their concerns were unfounded, perhaps they would allow her to return to the lab again.

She wasn't stupid. She knew they'd be pissed off at her for leaving. But she'd also experienced their brand of punishment. It certainly didn't encourage her to behave. She loved being naughty, wicked, wild. She felt like someone completely different with Price and Gunner, and she enjoyed being this new woman, wondering if she'd actually changed or if she'd just managed to find the person she was meant to be all along.

She gently closed her car door and started the engine, holding her breath lest Price and Gunner come racing out of the front door. No one appeared, so she put the car in drive and escaped.

Her commute took half the time as normal. There were far fewer cars on the road at this time of the morning. She used her fob to enter the building and headed upstairs. She narrowed her eyes when she passed her lab, discovering no crime-scene tape blocking her way. Her temper spiked. She knew it. The few girly movies she'd seen said that she should be angry at them for lying to her, but that seemed like a waste of emotion. She'd suspected the lie and now confirmed it. In the future she'd simply have to be more investigative with their statements.

Logic told her they believed they were protecting her. It touched her that they cared so much about her that they'd lie to keep her safe.

As she considered that, she re-evaluated. Maybe she was being led by her feelings. Because right now, her heart was telling her she was in love with Price and Gunner and she'd forgive them anything.

She shook her head and unlocked the door to her lab. Wow. She'd have to find time to analyze that feeling. Right now, she needed to put everything out of her mind and settle down to work.

She'd anticipated having at least four hours to work before her men found her. But two hours later, she heard a noise behind her. Anger didn't begin to describe the fire in Price's eyes when he opened the door to her lab and found her behind the counter.

She'd forgotten a hair tie, so she'd grabbed her trusty number twos to pull her hair away from her face. Their positions reminded her of the first time Price had stepped into her lab. Had that really only been a week ago?

Gunner followed Price into the room, a thunderous expression on his face.

"Hey," she said, forcing a lightness to her voice she hoped would calm them down. Clearly now that they could see she was safe and sound they would relax. Hopefully.

"What the fuck are you doing in here?" Price bellowed.

Deni took a small step back, a foolish response considering there was a counter between them. "No crime-scene tape." Two could play the annoyed game. Besides, maybe she could divert some of their anger by countering with a bit of her own.

Gunner stepped around Price. Deni appreciated his interference, his help as he placed himself between her and the grizzly bear. At least she did until he spoke.

"Goddammit, Deni. Do you have any idea the kind of hell you just put us through? When we woke up and found you gone, we thought someone had kidnapped you."

She hadn't considered that. Price's mansion was more secure than Fort Knox. Plus her car had been gone. "I guess I should have left a note." She wasn't used to answering to anyone about her plans. This relationship stuff was going to take some getting used to. While she was taking the learning curve into account on their behalf, her lovers didn't appear to be doing the same.

"You think?" Price's voice was laced with complete and utter fury.

"I'm sorry. I didn't realize you'd be so upset. I assumed you'd wake up and realize where I was."

Gunner ran his hand through his hair and she took a moment to study his face. He was pale and panicked. Price didn't look much better.

She felt like shit. She walked around the corner and stepped closer to them. "I'm so, so sorry."

Gunner reached out and pulled her into his arms, hugging

her so tightly she couldn't breathe. She received a second's reprieve to suck in some air when he released her. Then it was driven away again when Price offered the same, strong embrace.

She loved them. That realization had been niggling at the back of her mind for days, but for the first time, she understood that they loved her too.

She smiled when Price dropped his arms. Her sunny expression caught them unaware as they both gave her a funny look. She wasn't able to put her feelings in words yet. Besides her parents, she'd never told anyone she loved them.

"This is our fault," Gunner said, glancing over at Price. "You're right, Deni. We were lying about the crime-scene division locking down your lab. I think maybe we should have stressed how real the danger surrounding you is."

Gunner walked over to her laptop and produced a flash drive from his pocket.

Price frowned. "Gunner, I thought—"

"No. She has a right to know what she's up against. Maybe if we'd told her from the beginning, this morning's nightmare wouldn't have happened."

Deni walked over to the computer. Gunner clicked a few keys and pulled up a file marked Top Secret. "We think you're being targeted by a very dangerous man."

Deni saw a picture of the Reverend, the man who'd engaged her in a rather heated debate, flash on to the screen. "That's him. The Reverend. But I thought he was just a suspect?"

Gunner shrugged. "He's our number one suspect, and my gut says he's the guy. His real name is James Leopold."

"Ordained?" she asked.

Gunner shook his head. "Not in any church we can find."

"I knew it."

Gunner used the mouse to scroll down the screen, revealing more information. "Apparently the Reverend James Leopold believes himself to be a prophet, a precursor to the arrival of the four horsemen of the apocalypse. He is offering human kind their last chance for salvation."

"You're kidding?" Deni asked. "He's a nut job."

"Scoff if you want, but this man has amassed quite a following, a devout congregation willing to clean up society according to his dictates. He had a rather lengthy agenda until the two of you had your run-in at the Boston Public Library. Since then, he's decided that the root of all evil stems from your research, pardon the pun. And you are the devil in disguise. He's become fixated on you."

Price leaned forward. "Prior to your lecture at the library, his followers had been arrested for causing disturbances outside abortion clinics. They had pissed off a slew of people when they picketed a gay rights assembly and protested at the funeral of several soldiers who'd been killed in the line of duty. They were a menace and their actions targeted quite a few groups. Now the man has narrowed his agenda. You."

"Who would follow someone so unhinged?"

Price tilted his head. "Unfortunately what the Reverend lacks in intelligence, he makes up for in public-speaking skills. He's quite the persuasive orator. According to my source, Leopold could talk a starving man into giving up his last breadcrumb."

Deni wasn't impressed. "So what am I supposed to do? Hide in your mansion until he forgets about me? If he's as crazy as you say, that could take quite a long time."

Gunner tapped his fingers on the desk, a sure sign that he was frustrated. "For right now, we play the legal game. I've filed for a restraining order. He can't call or come near you. He's forbidden from making any contact with you at all."

"Terrific, but I haven't seen him since the disturbance at my lecture."

Price crossed his arms. "We believe he's fueling the anger against you among his congregation. You said the harassing phone calls were from a woman, right?"

She nodded.

Gunner clicked off one file and opened another. "The FBI lifted some prints from the bomb and on other items in your apartment. They ran them through the computer and came up with two matches late yesterday. Agent Young emailed me this information last night." Gunner showed her the picture of a man and woman.

"I've never seen those people before in my life."

"Yeah. We figured as much. They're a married couple and members of the Reverend's church. The FBI is picking them up today for questioning. We're hoping they'll say they were acting under the Reverend's orders."

Price grunted. "I wouldn't hold my breath on that."

Deni agreed. "They won't sell him out if they genuinely believe that he's offering them salvation."

"Maybe. Maybe not. Agent Young can be very persuasive. We'll just have to see if they value their freedom over the saving of their souls. Plea bargains can be very tempting when threatened by years of incarceration."

"Do you know Chester Cook?" Price asked.

Deni nodded. "The night custodian? Sure. He's a nice old man, little odd, bit quiet. Why?"

Price ran his hand through her hair. He looked troubled. "He hasn't returned to work since the night of Curtis's shooting. My source says Chester is a member of the Reverend's congregation as well."

"You think he shot Curtis?"

Gunner took over the explanation. "You spend lots of

nights here in the lab, Deni. The night custodian would know that. You said yourself Curtis had never slept here. When we found Curtis, his face was turned away from the door. I think we can assume Chester opened the door and fired, confident he was harming his intended victim."

"Me," she whispered.

"That's why we were so frantic when we realized your car was gone. Our fears turned from kidnapping to the idea that you were here and Chester could get to you."

Her heart broke at Price's admission. "But you said he's gone."

"There's a warrant out for his arrest, but so far the police have had no luck in finding him. He could be anywhere. If he felt strongly enough to try to kill you once, what's to stop him again?"

Deni's chest tightened with a fear so blinding she was afraid she'd fall down. Too much had happened in too short a time period. Shock and panic were warring for control inside her. "Does that restraining order you requested apply to the Reverend's entire congregation too? You know…that huge group of people who are apparently willing to do his bidding?" She didn't try to hide the quiver in her voice.

Gunner frowned, recognizing her fear. "I didn't say it was the answer to the problem. It's just a hoop we're jumping through in order to build a case against the man. We're going to keep you safe, Deni. You have to believe that."

"I'm sorry." She felt guilty for snapping at him. She just hated living this way. After a lifetime of nothing special, she was suddenly thrust into a world of absolute bliss and unquestionable terror. The extremes were starting to wear her out.

Price reached over and grasped her hand. "We're going to get this guy, Denise. He'll slip up somewhere and then we'll have him. He's going to pay for what he's done to you. To Curtis."

The mention of her assistant's name sent tears to her eyes. "It's my fault he was shot."

"Oh, hell no." Price tugged on her hand, pulling her into his arms. "Don't you dare go there. Leopold hurt Curtis. Not you."

Deni wrapped her arms around his waist, soaked up the strength of his embrace, let it ground her, calm her. "I'm not waiting for him to make a mistake."

Gunner narrowed his eyes. "What?"

"I think we should draw the Reverend out into the open. Lure the beast from his lair."

Price shook his head. "Hell no."

"Think about it. Right now, we're always on the defensive, trying to sidestep his attacks. We're not in control. He is. We'll never win this way. If we set a trap, one that's too tempting for Leopold to resist, suddenly we're holding the cards."

Gunner pushed away from the desk. "Absolutely not."

Deni looked from Gunner to Price and knew she'd never win this argument with logic. She'd have to fight dirty. "Fine. Then I'll go to the Grand Master and refuse this match. Tell him I'm no longer interested in being a member of the Trinity Masters."

Price reared back as if she'd hit him. "Why would you do that? You'd lose everything."

"I already have. Let's face it. I'm sitting on a big pile of nothing right now. I can't continue my research. I've lost my freedom. And I don't have your trust." It was a low blow, but it had the desired effect.

Gunner grasped her hands. "That's not true."

"How long have you known about Leopold?"

Gunner flushed, glanced over at Price uneasily.

Price shrugged once, the action filled with guilt. "Five days."

She knew that answer, but it didn't make his admission hurt any less. "Why didn't you tell me?"

"We didn't want you to be scared, Denise."

"You didn't trust me enough to tell me the truth. You tried to hide it from me. I'm just a child in your eyes. Some little doll for you to play with and coddle. I won't live like that."

Gunner's face reflected pure misery. She hated hurting them, but she refused to put their future on hold, be held prisoner according to the whims of a madman.

"That's not true, Deni."

"Prove it. Trust me enough to do what I'm asking."

Price frowned. "You're not leaving us much of a choice."

"So you'll help me set a trap?"

Neither man moved for several moments, and then they both slowly nodded.

PRICE STOOD at the entrance of the Boston Public Library three weeks later and cursed himself for being such a lovesick, fucking fool. Denise had pressured him into this farce with her threat to leave him, and he'd reacted with his emotions rather than his brain. That never happened.

"Is the sound working?" Gunner's voice broadcast through his earpiece. Price glanced toward the stage where the other man stood and nodded.

They'd begrudgingly agreed to participate in Denise's trap, though it had taken them some time to put all the pieces in place. Denise had moved her research to their home—he'd stopped thinking of it as his house weeks ago—and set up a makeshift lab in a small cottage just outside the main house. His father had built the cottage for his mother, who used to enjoy writing poetry. Price's mother would spend hours in the quaint little house, letting the peace and solitude of the place fuel her muse.

Denise seemed to have fallen in love with the cottage as well. He'd never met a more devoted or harder worker in his life. While the three of them lost themselves in lust for hours each evening, Denise never failed to rise with the birds, heading to her lab to run her trials and experiments for hours on end.

Gunner had secured a permanent transfer to the Boston office, returning to D.C. for several days to pack up his apartment and office. They'd just finished unpacking the last of Gunner's things two nights earlier, most of his belongings being absorbed into the large house, while a few things—unneeded furniture—was sold or given away.

Now that both of his lovers were living in the house, Price wondered how he'd spent so many years in the huge rambling mansion alone. Gunner, a music lover, was always blasting his collection of classic rock, while their absent-minded Denise was forever losing a shoe or her comb. Once she'd actually misplaced her toothbrush, and they'd spent nearly an hour looking for it. They'd found it in a jar of pencils on her desk.

They had decided to try to lure the Reverend out into the open by widely advertising another lecture on the importance of stem-cell research given by Dr. Denise Parker. Denise's first talk had lured Leopold out, so they hoped this one would as well. They'd sweetened the pot by adding that the lecture would be held as part of a fundraising effort for the laboratory. The newspaper reported that several top politicians in the area would attend. The Grand Master had friends in high places and he'd pledged to help Price in his attempts to lure the madman into the open.

For three weeks, Price had his top men at Bennett Securities working closely with Gunner's friends at the FBI. They'd gone over schematics of the library—most specifically the Rabb Lecture Hall, where Denise would speak—pinpointing key places in the auditorium that needed to be covered. Price had purchased bulletproof material for the podium as well as a thin Kevlar vest that Denise was currently wearing under her suit jacket. Gunner would be in position near her on the stage, while Price would cover things from the back, watching the audience from above. Three of Price's best men, as well as Agent Young, would be stationed at various places around the auditorium, though they would be dressed in plain clothes and acting as members of the audience. They decided it would be best if they maintained the appearance of a low-security event.

Given that most of the Reverend's past attempts on Denise had been instituted through the use of other people, they were on high alert, well aware that the threat could come from anyone. Price wasn't sure if he should hope for the man's arrival or not. He'd become accustomed to Denise working from home. He liked the peace of mind that provided him. He and Gunner had begun taking turns working from home, ensuring that one of them was always close by during the day.

The doors to the auditorium opened and people began filing in. Price heard Gunner mutter, "show time," through the earpiece. Price tried to remain calm, but an uneasy feeling crept in. He began to question their decisions, second-guessing everything. The lecture hall was on the lower concourse, which meant they would have to climb stairs to reach the nearest exit. That had been his main concern when they chose this room, but he'd let Gunner assure him they had the stairs secured and that Denise would have easy access to it from the door at stage right. Men were in position at the top and the bottom of the stairwell and his limousine was parked right outside the exit,

Roman instructed to keep the motor running and to be ready to leave quickly if needed.

"We've got a big crowd of protestors forming up here." Price recognized Pearson's voice coming through his earpiece. Pearson was one of his top employees and Price didn't like to acknowledge the man's anxious tone.

"Stay in position. Keep them out of the library," Price said into the microphone tucked in the lapel of this jacket.

Gunner and Denise were standing in front of the stage, speaking to the lab director and the mayor. Denise's boss was unaware of the trap, so it was important Denise play her part.

For the director, this lecture was the kickoff of a huge fundraising campaign. Price had already promised to make a large contribution to the lab should things take a bad turn. Hell, he'd make the donation regardless. After weeks spent with Denise, he'd come to understand exactly how vital her work was.

The auditorium was nearly full when Pearson spoke again. "Local police have arrived. It's getting crazy up here."

Before Price could respond, a fire detector went off. Glancing toward the door, Price saw smoke drifting under the door.

Someone else noticed too. "Fire!"

Panic ensued as everyone in the auditorium rose, clamoring for the exit. Price caught only a brief glimpse of Gunner as he grabbed Denise and pushed her toward the side exit.

Price fought his way against the tide of terrified people, waiting until he saw Gunner get her safely out of the auditorium. Then he took off for the staircase. He'd meet them at the top and together they'd get Denise out. As he reached the stairs, he glanced down in time to see Gunner and Denise turn a corner. Before they could begin climbing, Gunner roughly shoved Denise forward.

Time stood still as a shot rang out. Price sprinted down the steps, desperate to reach his lovers. Gunner's body flew back, slamming against a wall just as Price grasped Denise.

"Get her out of here," Gunner yelled. Price's gaze met Gunner's and a lifetime of understanding passed between them in those split seconds. Price nodded and turned Denise, pushing her up.

"No!" Denise tried to go back to Gunner, so Price lifted her, tossing her over his shoulder as he ran up the stairs.

"Stop! Gunner's hurt. We have to go back! We have to go back!" Her fists beat on his back as smoke burned his eyes, but Price didn't stop. He had one goal. The limo.

The bright sunlight pierced his vision as they burst through a side door. Mercifully, the limo was in place. Price ran to the car and threw open the door.

Denise was crying. "We have to get Gunner."

He tossed her onto the seat. "I'll go back, Denise. I'll get him and we'll meet you at home."

"Please." Her voice trembled through her tears.

"I'll get him. He'll be okay. I promise." He prayed to God that was a promise he would be able to keep. Slamming the car door, he pounded on the roof twice, indicating for Roman to take off. The car pulled away from the curb quickly.

Before Price could turn to return to the library, he spotted a man lying in the middle of the street right next to where the limo had been parked. Roman.

Price started to run to his driver just as Gunner emerged through the side door.

"What the fuck?" Gunner said, hot on Price's heels.

They reached Roman together and helped the man to his feet. "That man, the Reverend. He tricked me out of the car."

Price glanced down the street in time to see the limo take a left turn, its progress hindered by the growing crowd of protestors. Price didn't bother to consider his actions. He simply took off.

Gunner was right beside him, step for step. A quick look told him his friend had indeed been shot, but given the strong, determined expression on Gunner's face, his injury didn't appear to be too bad. When they reached the corner, they spotted the limousine as it turned down a side alley.

"That alley is a dead end," Price said.

Gunner pointed to the people blocking the street. "Looks like the Reverend didn't realize his plan to distract us would cut off his only means of escape."

Price pointed to the bar on the corner. "I'll go through the bar, come at him from the side. You block the end of the alley. We'll trap him."

Price entered the bar, ignoring the bartender who asked if he wanted a drink. He walked down a long corridor, past the bathrooms and a storeroom until he found the exit that would lead him to the alley.

He slid the door open slowly, taking in the horrifying scene before him. The Reverend had his back to Price. He held Denise in front of him as he pressed a knife to her throat. Gunner tossed his gun onto the ground at Leopold's command.

Price raised his weapon but hesitated to fire. Given his angle, if the bullet should pass through Leopold, it would go into Denise. Price kept the gun trained on the Reverend's back, waiting for his moment.

Soon enough, it came.

Leopold kicked Gunner's weapon under the limo and then turned to his side as he passed the FBI man. All the Reverend's attention was focused on Gunner. Denise was considerably shorter than Leopold. She was slumped, clearly determined to make the villain drag her. She wasn't helping the man's escape and her position offered Price a clean shot.

The Reverend never saw Price step into the alleyway, take aim and fire. His bullet went straight through Leopold's head. Gunner grabbed Denise as the man fell. When Price reached them, Denise was running her hands over Gunner's shoulder, trying to apply pressure to the bleeding there.

"Gunner's been shot." Her eyes when she looked at Price were glazed, unfocused. Shock was beginning to set in.

Price nodded. "I know. We'll take care of it."

He jerked when he heard footsteps coming down the alley. Price raised his weapon and then lowered it as Agent Young approached.

Young took in the scene. "Leopold dead?"

Price started to laugh at the inane question. The man was lying in a pool of his own blood and brain matter. Instead, he said, "yeah."

Young pointed to the weapon in Price's hand. "Is that the gun that did it?"

Price hesitated. While he knew Gunner trusted the fellow FBI agent, Price still wasn't sure what to make of the man.

Gunner answered. "Yeah. That's it."

Young's gaze traveled over Gunner as he sat on the ground, Denise in his arms, her trembling hands trying to stem the flow of blood. "You okay?"

Gunner nodded.

"Why don't the three of you get out of here? Get yourself stitched up. I'll clear the scene."

Gunner rose on unsteady feet. He'd lost a fair amount of blood and it was clear the adrenaline that had sent him chasing after Denise was fading fast. Price stepped closer and placed a strong hand under his friend's arm to help him.

"Take the limo," Young suggested. "And I'll need that gun."

Price didn't hand the weapon over until Gunner placed a

hand on his shoulder. "It's okay, Price. Young knows what he's doing."

Price gave the agent the gun, opened the door of the limo and helped Gunner and Deni inside. He walked to the front, relieved to find the keys still hanging in the ignition. He really didn't want to have to rummage through a dead man's pants for them.

Putting the car in reverse, he slowly maneuvered out of the alley. The crowd on the street had dispersed, though there were still quite a few patrol cars parked in front of the library, their lights flashing.

He glanced in the rearview mirror. "Where to?"

Denise instantly said, "The hospital."

Price didn't acknowledge her response. He knew where she wanted to go.

Gunner held his gaze through the reflection. "You know how to stitch?"

"Yeah."

"You got supplies at the mansion?"

Price nodded. "I do."

"Then let's go home."

Deni started to protest, but Price let Gunner explain why it was better for them to lay low. Young's job of cleaning up the mess they'd left would be that much harder if an FBI agent arrived at the hospital with a hole in his arm.

Silence fell in the limo as exhaustion took over.

Only one thought managed to penetrate Price's hazy mind, repeating itself like a mantra.

We made it. We made it.

We made it.

CHAPTER EIGHT

"Young," Gunner said, shaking hands with his new partner. His boss at the FBI had decided he and Agent Young made a good team. He'd just gotten the new orders this morning that they would work together.

"How are you holding up, partner?"

Gunner grinned. "Looks like you're stuck with me."

Young shrugged. "I can think of worse guys to work with. How's the arm?"

Gunner pulled a chair out from the table and sat. He gestured for Young to join him. His arm was bandaged up, but Gunner refused to wear a sling. It ached like the devil, but today was too important and there was no way in hell he'd show up looking injured.

He'd asked Young to meet with him in the library. Two days had passed since he'd seen the agent in the alley. Gunner and Price had kept Deni at home following her wild ride in the limo with the Reverend. Deni, in typical form, had bounced back quickly from the frightening event. While she'd cried herself to sleep the first night, by the next morning she was more like her old self, laughing with them over breakfast. The second night had been easier as they had playful sex in the hot tub, all of them grateful that they were still alive, still together.

He glanced at his watch. "I've only got a few minutes. I'm sorry I haven't had a chance to talk to you since the shooting."

Agent Young grinned. "Well, I don't blame you there. If I had a pretty nurse like your Dr. Parker, I wouldn't bother to come up for air either."

Gunner rolled his eyes, but he was glad to see Young had jumped to the conclusion he, Price and Deni had agreed upon. There was a brief article in the newspaper regarding the protest at the library, followed up by a slew of articles about the importance of stem-cell research. The lab director had called Deni this morning to tell her that contributions to the lab had already doubled the previous year's campaign. Gunner suspected Price had written a fairly large check as well.

Young had outdone himself suppressing the truth from the media. The so-called fire at the library was falsely reported as smoke bombs set off by prankster teenagers. But the true masterpiece was the explanation of the Reverend's death.

"So Leopold killed himself?" Gunner asked.

Young nodded. "Got drunk in that bar on the corner, walked out into the alley and put a gun to the side of his head. Several patrons of the bar have reported overhearing him talk about the fact he was a fraud and he was about to be exposed."

Gunner appreciated the man's ingenuity. Young would have made an excellent member of the Trinity Masters. "Smart. It's harder for his followers to make him a martyr if he reveals himself as a liar and takes his own life."

Young straightened his tie. "That's what I thought. We've also leaked some details about his early life, his time spent in a sanatorium, his run-ins with the law, questions that have been raised about how he got his money through illegal means."

"What about his congregation?"

"Word on the street says they're disbanding. A lot of the higher ups, Leopold's trusted friends, are vanishing, lying low until everything dies down."

Gunner rubbed his arm, trying to ignore the twinge of pain. "What about the guy who shot me?"

"It was the night custodian at the lab, Chester Cook. The same guy who shot Deni's assistant, Curtis."

Gunner recalled seeing the man knocked down through the haze of smoke in the stairwell. "One of Bennett's guys tackled him right after he shot me."

"Yeah. The security guard was still holding him when the police got there. Told them he was the guy wanted for questioning in Curtis's attack. Good thing Price had the foresight to flash Cook's picture around to his staff along with the Reverend's when we were setting up the sting operation. Helped us kill two birds with one stone. Once Cook heard about the Reverend's suicide, he sang like a canary, confessed everything."

"Good."

Young frowned. "What's the deal with you and that Bennett guy anyway?"

Gunner grinned, deciding to use one of Price's favorite phrases. "I could tell you, but I'd have to kill you."

Young rolled his eyes as Gunner rose.

"I appreciate the way you took care of everything, Young."

The man shrugged, obviously uncomfortable by the praise. Then he stood too. "What are you all dressed up for?"

It was the first time Young had acknowledged Gunner's formal suit. "I have a date. And I'm going to be late if I don't leave right now. See you at work."

He and Young shook hands, then Gunner headed for the

rare-book room. A month had passed since the introduction ceremony.

What a month.

Today was the formal binding ceremony. He was about to be joined with Price Bennett and Denise Parker for the rest of his life.

Gunner grinned. He couldn't wait.

A FEW HOURS and one ceremony later, Gunner entered the limo first, reaching back to help Deni in. She was giggling, her face gleaming with pure joy.

Price stood at the door with Roman, who was also sporting stitches. While Gunner's were in his arm, Roman's were on the back of his head. It turned out the driver had been lured from the limo the day of the lecture when he witnessed a thug knock an old lady down and steal her purse. Roman had jumped from the vehicle to help the woman up when someone bashed him on the head from behind. He'd been unconscious in the middle of the road until the limo pulled away from the curb.

"Take the scenic route," Gunner heard Price instruct the driver. Roman winked and nodded as Price climbed in and shut the door.

"We did it. We're married." Deni's smile grew even wider.

It was a contagious look. Gunner couldn't contain his happiness either. "You're right. We are."

Price stretched his arm along the backseat, tugging Deni closer. Gunner had claimed the side couch as usual.

"I think we need to go on a honeymoon," Price said.

Deni laughed. "We've been honeymooning for the past month."

Price shrugged. "I want more. Besides, I mean a real honeymoon. I want to go somewhere. I own a small island in the

Caribbean that would be perfect. It's very secluded and private. No one would—"

Deni and Gunner burst into loud peals of laughter.

"You own an island?" Gunner wasn't sure why he was surprised. In the past month, he'd discovered Price owned several restaurant chains, a private jet and a home on Martha's Vineyard.

Price wasn't deterred. "I'll make the arrangements with my personal assistant."

When Price wanted something, he got it. Gunner suspected that would cause waves somewhere down the road, but for now, he didn't want to worry about the future. He was more interested in the here and now.

"You look beautiful in that dress, Deni."

She blushed, looking down at the silky white slip dress. "I feel sort of silly in it. I don't wear dresses very often."

Gunner moved toward her, knelt on the floor at her feet and opened her legs with his hands on her knees. "That's a shame. Makes it awfully easy for me to do this." He reached out, pushed the thin layer of her panties aside and pressed two fingers inside her hot, wet sex.

Her eyes drifted closed and she sighed contentedly. "Maybe I should add a few more dresses to my wardrobe."

Gunner added another finger. "Maybe you should."

Price turned in his seat slightly, watching in silence as Gunner finger-fucked their wife.

"Deni," Gunner said when her face began to flush, her hips thrusting against him, seeking more friction. He waited until her eyes opened and focused on him. "I want you."

She nodded.

Gunner reached for her, lifted her from the seat until she also knelt on the floor. He directed her between Price's outstretched legs. Price had freed his cock while Gunner fingered Deni. When he recognized Gunner's plan, Price lifted his hips and shoved his pants to his ankles.

"I want you to suck Price's cock while I fuck you from behind."

Deni nodded eagerly. They'd yet to discover any game their little virgin scientist wasn't willing to play. Deni bent over the seat and wrapped her hand around the base of Price's dick.

Gunner tugged on her hips, spreading her ass cheeks with his thumbs. "So fucking pretty."

Gunner let go just long enough to release himself from his own constricting pants. Price's sharp intake of breath caught his attention and he watched Deni's lips move along Price's erect flesh before parting to suck the head in deep on the first pass.

"Fuck." Price reached for the silver hair sticks he'd bought her as a wedding present, pulled them out and freed Deni's thick blonde waves. His fingers tangled in Deni's tresses, tightening, using his grip to drive her mouth faster.

Gunner couldn't resist any longer. He placed his cock at the opening of her sex and shoved deep with one rough thrust.

Deni groaned and mimicked his impatient rhythm. All the finesse of the past month disappeared as the three of them moved together in sheer primal passion. Gunner fucked her hard, pounding into her tight pussy, his fingers leaving marks on her hips at his tight grip.

Price began to mumble a mantra of curse words as Deni sucked his dick faster. "Fuck, fuck, fuck. Oh, fuck yeah, baby."

Deni's climax struck the same time as Gunner's. They both jerked and tensed as he filled her with jet after jet of hot come. Exhausted, he withdrew and fell to his haunches.

Deni had released Price's cock as she came. When she reached out to resume her blowjob, he tilted her face up and shook his head.

Then he lifted her and placed her knees on either side of his hips. "Ride me, beautiful."

Deni took his cock inside her sex and started to bounce. Price tugged at the zipper on the back of her dress and pulled the straps over her shoulders. Deni didn't wear a bra. Gunner moved closer, planting himself between Price's legs.

As Price took Deni's breast into his hand and lifted it to his lips, Gunner decided he wanted back in the game.

He ran his finger around Deni's sex, feeling as Price's thick cock pressed into her. He gathered up some of the moisture there, coating his finger with it. Then he pushed the tip into her anus.

Deni stilled as he forged farther. Without lube, he wouldn't dare take her with more than a single finger. Deni genuinely liked anal sex and they'd both claimed her that way often. Even so, they had never been careless, never failed to prepare her properly, to make sure the act was one they could all enjoy.

Once his finger was completely lodged, he wiggled it playfully, relishing the sound of her breathless laugh. Then Gunner indicated for her to continue her movements on top of Price. Deni had only started thrusting on Price once more when Gunner realized he had more to give.

Reaching down with his free hand, he cupped Price's balls firmly.

Price's head flew back against the seat. "Holy fuck."

Gunner didn't halt his assault. He was in this far, he might as well keep going. He continued to apply pressure to Price's balls as Deni bounced on his cock. Gunner added more fuel to the flame burning inside Deni as he started fucking her ass with his finger.

Time stood still as they each reached for their climax, wild animals seeking satiation and not caring how they got it. Price came first, his fingers tightening on Deni's waist. Then Deni screamed out her release before collapsing against Price's chest.

Gunner didn't move from his place on the floor, though he removed his hands from his lovers.

Price's gaze captured his and held it. Then Price slowly nodded. Gunner understood. Maybe not tonight, hell, maybe not even this year, but somewhere down the road, he and Price would be mapping a new path, one unlike anything either of them had ever experienced.

Deni lifted her head, glancing at Gunner over her shoulder. She shifted off Price's lap, claimed the center of the backseat and beckoned Gunner to join them.

She took both of their hands in hers and Gunner wondered at the sudden seriousness on her face.

"I just wanted to say that I love you. Both of you. I've never really said that to anyone, and I know you both sort of got stuck with me, but I was hoping maybe you…"

Her voice faded away, and Gunner realized she actually looked worried that they didn't feel the same way.

Gunner squeezed her hand and turned her face toward his with a finger on her chin. "I love you too, Deni. So much it hurts sometimes. You're my friend, my lover. My wife. I feel so lucky to have you in my life."

A smile covered her face as he bent to kiss her. It was a slow, sweet, gentle melding of lips. He hoped she'd be able to feel the truth of his words through the touch.

As they parted, Price was there. He reached for her and pulled their petite lover onto his large lap. "I think I first started to fall in love with you at the lab the day we met. You were a white-hot mess with those safety glasses hanging on your nose, the pencils in your hair, the dead cellphone in your purse. Deep inside, I couldn't help but think this woman needs me. And I need her. I lived most of my life dating perfect women.

Women with classic beauty, poise, flawless manners, the right upbringing—"

"Wow. This took a bad turn," Deni teased.

Price grinned. "What I'm saying is, I thought they were perfect because of all those superficial, stupid things. The fact is you're the perfect one."

Deni smiled. "Perfect is a hell of a lot better than special."

Price laughed. "You're both. And more. God, Denise. You're everything to me."

She wiped her eyes, not bothering to hide the tears their words had produced. Gunner had come to recognize her happy crying. "You both said that a lot better than me."

Gunner grinned. "It's not a contest. It'll never be that between us."

"Just love?" she asked.

Gunner nodded. "And laughter. And maybe half a dozen kids."

"And lots of games of hide and seek," Price added.

Deni wrapped her arms around both of their necks and pulled them closer until the three of them were only a breath away from each other. "I love you. Now, how soon until we can head to the island?"

EPILOGUE

The Grand Master walked down the long corridor and released a sigh of relief. The triad of Price, Gunner and Deni had caused him a few sleepless nights as he considered how much could be lost if things didn't go well. Seeing them today at the binding ceremony, recognizing the unmistakable love in their eyes, had set his mind at ease.

He entered his chambers, walked to his desk and sat. Before he could call the next trinity to the altar, there was a member in need of help. Marco Polin and Damon Corzo had been playing with fire for years. College friends, they'd joined the Trinity Masters together and then used the fact that they would one day be placed in an arranged-marriage ménage as an excuse to indulge.

Marco was a world famous cello player who had done more to make classical music sexy than anyone in the past hundred years. Damon had been groomed for law practically from childbirth and was one of the youngest partners in a heavy-hitting international firm. In a few more years, he would be a judge and in a prime position to help further the vision of the Trinity Masters.

But Damon was being blackmailed. His predilection for sharing pretty women—sometimes two or three at a time—with Marco had caught up with them. Photos of the two of them and some showgirls romping on a bed in Vegas had been delivered to Damon with a demand for a million dollars.

Unless the blackmailer could be found, Damon would never sit on the bench, and Marco's career, which was built on the back of the courtly love of the world's women, would be over, eliminating an important artistic voice.

But catching a blackmailer was no easy thing. There was only one Trinity Master who might be able to do it.

The Grand Master opened the file. Tasha Kash, born Natasha Kasharin, daughter of Russian spies, was a secret weapon of the United States government both abroad and domestically, and possibly the most dangerous member of the Trinity Masters.

The Grand Master had served as the leader of this secret society for nearly a decade, inheriting the position from his father. In all those years, he'd yet to make a match that didn't take.

While that track record was impressive, it was also frightening. With each successful match, he felt more and more pressure to succeed.

And this next triad may be the riskiest one ever.

Don't stop now! The Grand Master is about the create another trinity. Scorching Desire is available now.

. . .

READ THE ENTIRE TRINITY MASTERS: Fall of the Grand Master
  Elemental Pleasure
  Primal Passion
  Scorching Desire
  Forbidden Legacy

AND CHECK out these other series...all part of the Trinity Masters world.

SECRETS AND SIN
  Hidden Devotion
  Elegant Seduction
  Secret Scandal
  Delicate Ties
  Beloved Sacrifice
  Masterful Truth

MASTERS ADMIRALTY
  Treachery's Devotion
  Loyalty's Betrayal
  Pleasure's Fury
  Honor's Revenge
  Bravery's Sin

THE HAYDEN BROTHERS
  Fiery Surrender
  Necessary Pursuit

Joyful Engagement (a novella)
Wrath's Storm

THE MAFIA
Suspicion's Fire
Desire's Addiction
Danger's Heir

WARRIOR SCHOLARS
Hollywood Lies

CALLING ALL FACEBOOK FANS! Did you know there's a group for fans of the Trinity Masters series? Come join Mari and Lila for behind-the-scenes stories, contests, exclusive sneak peeks, and hilarious text threads. Join the society right HERE.

CLICK to the next page to read the prologue of Scorching Desire.

SCORCHING DESIRE

 hapter One

He'd put them all in danger.

Damon put his hand in his pocket and formed a fist, trying to hide his anger. He had no one to be angry at but himself.

"You understand what's at stake." The Grand Master sat in shadow, only his right hand, which lay on the desk, visible. They were in the secret headquarters of the Trinity Masters, deep under the Boston library.

"I do, Grand Master." Damon couldn't stand still. He paced the private office. "I'll resign."

"And how will that benefit the Trinity Masters?"

"I'll resign from everything, including the Trinity Masters."

"Mr. Corzo, I think you forget who we are. You do not leave the Trinity Masters."

Damon turned away, examining the shadowy corners of

the office. The Trinity Masters were America's oldest and most powerful secret society. Formed as the states were uniting in rebellion, the first leaders sought to strengthen their new nation through alliances between powerful and important people. They used the arranged marriages to connect influential families, captains of industry and religious leaders. But it wasn't just two people they united, it was three.

In modern times, becoming a member meant access to some of the most powerful and innovative thinkers in the country. If you were selected to join you were guaranteed to rise far and fast. The Trinity Masters counted politicians, CEOs, Nobel Prize winning scientists and world-renowned artists among their ranks. The Grand Master of the Trinity Masters helped the members excel in their chosen profession or field, and when the time came, he called them to the altar and matched them with two others in a trinity marriage.

At twenty-seven, Damon was already an Assistant U.S. Attorney, the third step in a six-part fifteen-year plan to put him on the federal bench. He'd joined the Trinity Masters in college. It hadn't made his life easier. Instead, it had pushed him to work harder, to excel each step of the way.

And knowing that he would someday be part of an arranged marriage meant he had taken full advantage of the fact he didn't need to worry about dating or relationships.

That had led to his current problem.

"Your friendship with Marco Polin was unusual, but not problematic." The Grand Master tapped his fingers on the top of his desk. "Until now."

"I know, Grand Master."

"There are several legal options." Damon rubbed his eyebrow. "But almost all of them would then require the video be entered into evidence. We could try to limit access to the evidence. The likelihood that anyone who sees the video would make the connection between Marco and I and the Trinity—"

"Is an unacceptable risk. Your rings are clearly visible. It would be far too easy for someone to start wondering why an Assistant U.S. Attorney and a famous cellist were wearing matching rings while they fucked the same woman."

Damon hung his head.

Taking advantage of his freedom until he was called to the altar had included indulging in every sexual desire and kink that ever interested him. His job required him to be circumspect with his personal life. But luckily, Marco Polin—a college friend who was also in the Trinity Masters—was a famous musician with the elegant playboy lifestyle that only classical musicians could pull off. For years Damon had been attending Marco's parties, which had the tendency to devolve into orgies, to indulge himself.

This time they'd been caught on tape. The blackmail video had shown up in his personal email three days ago. He'd immediately gotten in touch with the Grand Master, who'd ordered him to Boston.

"Tell me again, how many people were at the party?"

"When the video was taken? Ten, maybe. They were all women except for Marco and I."

"An enjoyable sex party."

"It wasn't like that..." The protest was lame. It had been exactly like that. It was hardly his fault that he enjoyed sexy, adventurous women. And when the one Marco was fucking had beckoned him over so she could suck his cock, who was he to stand in the way of a lady's pleasure?

"How did these women come to be at the party?"

"I'm not sure." Despite the seriousness of the situation, Damon's lips twitched. "Marco attracts beautiful women."

"This is risky behavior."

"Don't worry, we're both on the new experimental STD vaccines."

"How thrilling that you're taking advantage of your fellow Trinity Master's scientific advancements."

Damon was a respected and aggressive attorney, a fearless human-rights activist and an expert pugilist. The Grand Master made him feel like a stupid teenager.

"Grand Master, I deeply regret what I've done and the trouble it's caused you and the Trinity Masters. The blackmailer didn't mention the matching rings—they just want money. I'll quit the Trinity Masters and pay the blackmailer. I will, of course, still help you in any way you ask. I will remain a friend to the Trinity Masters."

The Grand Master picked up a letter opener and balanced it on the top of the desk. It didn't escape Marco that it was shaped like a sword.

"Many of our members have helped you get where you are today. I don't discount your abilities—you're unique in your passion and remarkable in your skills, but neither will I discount our efforts to accelerate your career. You would be a valuable addition to the justice system."

The Grand Master sat forward, his strong face visible by the light of the single desk lamp. Damon noticed just a trace of weariness in the man's eyes that surprised him. However, that brief sign of weakness was soon replaced with a hard expression that said the Grand Master would not be crossed.

"Perhaps you've forgotten why our society exists. We protect the United States, we ensure that the best and the brightest rise to protect the ideals of our great nation. You're part of that plan. We need you on the bench as a federal judge."

"Yes, Grand Master." Damon bowed his head.

"I will send someone to assist you with the situation. I expect your full attention until this is resolved."

"I have to be in court in ten days, sir."

"Then you have a deadline. I will contact you."

Damon looked at the Grand Master, waiting to hear what the plan was or who he would send to help them. From his time as a prosecutor and working in a private firm, Damon knew that blackmail was infamously unreported, precisely because by its very nature it meant that the victim couldn't, or wouldn't, go to the authorities. The situation would have been bad enough for him personally and professionally even without the added complication of his actions putting the secret of the Trinity Masters in jeopardy.

"Goodbye, Mr. Corzo."

Damon raised one brow. There was no mistaking that dismissal.

He made his way out of the Trinity Masters' headquarters, taking the secret elevator to the rare-book room in the back of the Boston Library. He pulled his phone from his pocket as he walked.

"Marco," he said when his friend picked up. "I just met with the GM. I'm coming to Chicago."

He booked a flight on his phone as he hailed a cab. All he could hope was that the Grand Master had some very good tricks up his sleeve.

The Grand Master swiveled his chair, staring into the shadows in the corner.

"Well?" he asked.

Natasha Kasharin stepped from the darkness into the light. She wore slim black pants and a white button-down shirt, which should have been simple, nearly androgynous attire. But she looked more sexual than another woman would in lingerie, and more dangerous than a Navy SEAL in full gear.

"You heard?" he asked her.

Natasha, who went by Tasha, cocked her head to the side, blonde hair falling against her cheek. "Blackmailed at an orgy? How original."

The Grand Master's lips twitched. Tasha was witty and fun, but few people had an opportunity to see it. Natasha's life had been anything but easy—her membership in the Trinity Masters was meant to correct that, to give her safety and a chance at a meaningful, if not exactly traditional, relationship.

Though she was American by birth, she was the daughter of two KGB agents and had been raised to be a spy for Russia. At the age of twelve she'd turned herself in to the CIA and spent high school as a double agent, reporting on her own parents' activities.

Her patriotism had come at a terrible cost, and when her CIA handler—a Trinity Masters member—retired, he'd helped Tasha get out of the spy business and made sure she became a member of their society.

The Grand Master had wanted to respect his old friend's request that Tasha be given a life worthy of her sacrifice, but she was too skilled and valuable a resource for him to ignore. In the five years since she'd been a member, she'd cleaned up messes, taken down those who stood in their way and retrieved information they needed.

He'd used her the same way her parents had. The same way the CIA had.

As much as he might want to stick to his ideals, the Grand Master couldn't ignore the sharpest weapon in his arsenal. There were men and women who were more dangerous, more powerful. They were guns—violent and hot, or knives—sharp and cold. Tasha was a syringe full of poison—silent, deadly and unnoticed until it was too late. And unlike the others he considered dangerous, Tasha had nothing to lose.

"I will talk to him first," she said. "He is lying about something."

"It wouldn't surprise me. He'll go to Chicago. Marco has a place there."

"The other man in the video?"

"Yes."

"Good, I will talk to both of them." She walked toward the door.

"Tasha."

"Yes?" She didn't turn, but her steps paused.

"Don't kill anyone."

She turned her head just enough for him to see the curve of her cheek. "There are so many things worse than death."

The Grand Master stared at the closed door of his office for a long time after she left.

ABOUT THE AUTHORS

Virginia native Mari Carr is a *New York Times* and *USA TODAY* bestseller of contemporary sexy romance novels. With over two million copies of her books sold, Mari was the winner of the Romance Writers of America's Passionate Plume for her novella, *Erotic Research*.

Join her newsletter so you don't miss new releases and for exclusive subscriber-only content. You can visit Mari's website at https://maricarr.com or email her at mari@maricarr.com.

Lila Dubois is an award winning author of erotic, paranormal and fantasy romance. Her book J is for..., the tenth book in the bestselling checklist series, won the 2019 National Readers' Choice Award. Additionally, she's been nominated for the RT Book Reviews Erotic Novella of the Year for Undone Rebel and the Golden Flogger.

Having spent extensive time in France, Egypt, Turkey, Ireland and England Lila speaks five languages, none of them (including English) fluently. Lila lives in California with her own Irish Farm Boy and loves receiving email from readers.

You can visit Lila's website at www.liladubois.net. She loves to hear from fans! Send an email to author@liladubois.net or join her newsletter.

Made in the USA
Las Vegas, NV
21 January 2026

39918070R00100